HARD SHIFT

KATE ALLENTON

Published by Coastal Escape Publishing

Discover other titles by Kate Allenton

www.kateallenton.com

Chapter 1

This sucks. Abigail Elizabeth Monroe shifted the ungodly stack of papers from one arm to the other. Filing was just one of the many boring duties in the description of the job that the temp agency had given her. The sounds of voices filled the large open office where men and women worked from cubicles. She'd held this job for two days. Not a record, but it was a start. Some of the employees talked about their weekends while sipping coffee as she walked by and others were talking about the latest football game they'd watched on TV. She might as well have been invisible to these people who didn't even bother to ask her name.

Abigail settled on top of a little stool

and placed the papers at her feet so she could start filing. Several papercuts and hours later, she sucked the blood away as she shoved the last filing cabinet shut. Her entire shift had come and gone. She stood with her hands on her hips and stretched the kinks out of her neck.

Laughter floated to her ears as a group of woman stood around, purses on their shoulders, deciding where they'd meet after work for drinks. When they turned and spotted Abigail, she froze.

"Hey," Carol called. She'd been the supervisor in charge of giving Abigail her duties for the day.

"Me?" Abigail asked, glancing over her shoulder to find no one else behind her.

"We were just debating where to go for drinks." The woman grinned.

Hope blossomed in Abigail's heart. Were they going to ask her to join them? Had someone finally grown a kind bone? "Yeah?"

Carol pointed over to her desk. "That stack isn't going to file itself."

And just as quickly as the idea and hope for acceptance had taken form, it vanished, shriveling and wilting away like flower petals on a cold winter's day. Carol led the giggling women out of the office. Not one bothered to glance back with even a morsel of pity.

It was official. Abigail's life sucked, and

worse than that, she'd hit rock bottom. It had started that morning years ago she'd found both of her parents murdered in a vicious home invasion. Her life had gone downhill ever since.

Abigail took one more look at the stack of papers and rolled her eyes. She didn't have time for self-pity. Her emotions weren't going to pay the bills. She grabbed her purse, leaving the stack for Monday.

"It's not going to file itself," Abigail said in a mocking tone as she headed to the elevator and jabbed the call button.

"We're going out for drinks," she continued, mocking Carol as she stepped into the empty elevator. When the doors opened to the garage, the disappointment welling up inside had slowed to a simmer.

"These people don't matter," she repeated to herself, keys in hand as she headed toward her car in the dimly lit garage. The concrete structure was eerie with no sunlight shining in. This morning she hadn't been able to find a parking spot because the place was so full. Now the cars sat few and far between.

A man whistled in the distance echoing through the concrete tomb, startling her to a stop. A shiver skirted down her spine as her gaze darted around the cars and shadows dancing on the wall. A killer could pop out from anywhere. Chewing her bottom lip, she stood frozen, debating whether to return to the building or move on to her car. Visions of her parents' bloodless and unmoving bodies on the living room floor flashed in her mind. Her whole body tensed.

When the elevator dinged behind her, and a group of men and women walked out, she finally let out the breath she'd been holding and continued on to her car. If someone were to attack, at least there would be others around to hear her screams, even if they didn't know who she was.

Her steps quickened into a walking run until she reached her car. She clicked the Fob and slid behind the wheel quickly locking the doors behind her before shoving the key into the ignition.

I'm safe, she repeated over and over in her head as she slowly rolled through the parking garage, her gaze darting into every corner to see if she could find the source of the whistling.

Abigail drove straight home and parked her car as close to the front of the apartment building as possible. Her neighborhood wasn't in the best part of town, but it wasn't the worst either. It was just a place she could afford. She slid out of the car and scanned the lot. A couple of teens she'd noticed before were the only ones loitering nearby. She took the stairs two at a time until she reached her third floor. The familiar old, musty scent of the worn-out carpet drifted to her nose, and the muscles in her shoulders started to ease as she stepped inside her apartment, throwing the deadbolt into place behind her.

"Home sweet home." She dropped her purse on the table and walked directly into the kitchen, making herself an iced tea while she started her frozen dinner in the microwave. This was her life. It wasn't glamorous, but it was hers.

Abigail settled in front of the television with her nuked, cardboard-tasting dinner and flicked the news on. A story about a woman flashed on the screen. "Another abduction?"

"This makes the third person to disappear in the last three days," the reporter stated in a serious tone. "This abduction occurred just hours earlier in the Dawson Cliff area. Local police and the Shifter Investigation Division are on the scene, blocking the area. At this time, it's unclear if the missing person was human or a member of the shifter community. Police are urging everyone to take extra precautions and watch your surroundings when by yourself or to travel in groups to be safe. If you have any information, please contact Crime Stoppers or the police department at (555) 221-4376."

"I bet the asshole whistles while he's

snatching them," she mumbled around her next bite of food and flipped the channel to a detective show instead. She loved a good mystery and watching bad guys being thrown in jail. The fact that police still couldn't explain how her parents had their blood drained, and the fact that they hadn't charged anyone with the murders, made her stomach churn. Someone, somewhere, knew something.

Abigail took her dishes into the kitchen and cleaned up after herself. She walked over to the sliding glass door and looked out at the little garden on her balcony. Night had settled in, the moon shielded behind a foggy sky. Thunder rolled as lightning flashed in the distance. A storm was brewing and headed their way. She went to pull the curtains closed and glanced down into the parking lot. The boys from earlier were gone. Two men were leaning against a black van with blacked-out windows. Each was smoking, neither speaking as they glanced casually around the lot. The larger of the two looked up and met her gaze as the last blind closed, blocking his view. She shivered before heading to the door and making sure she had locked it tight. She grabbed a bat from the hallway closet and took it into her room before changing and sliding into her nice warm bed. Closing her eyes, she tried to remember her father's face and her mom's laugh, clinging to happier times when they'd been alive. Slowly, sleep carried her away into a dream state.

****

Abigail's eyes flew open, and her heart raced. Fear gripped her body, and her muscles tensed. The man from the parking lot looked down on her. His lips tilted up in a smile as he held a rag over her nose and mouth. His leg pinned one of her arms while the other was being held down by large fingers digging into her skin. Unable to turn her head, she could only make out the faint outline of the other man in the room. She felt the sharp prick of a needle in her arm and tried to scream and pull her arm free from the unyielding restraints.

"Don't make this hard on yourself. Just breathe," he whispered.

Panic struck hold, and she sucked in deep breaths, hoping to prolong her life. The medicinal scent hit her in the gut, clogging her nose and dulling her senses.

The men's voices sounded clogged and distorted to her ears as they spoke back and forth, and her lids turned heavy as she fought to keep her eyes open. Her blinking slowed.

Her world turned dark, and the voices

in the room quieted as the blackness sucked her into its web, cloaking her in the void she feared.

She drifted in and out of consciousness to the sound of a beeping machine. Her eyes slid open into the darkened room. The machine hooked up to her beeped to the rhythm of her weak heartbeat. Bags of blood hung from a pole nearby, the line going into a port in her arm. She felt a prick in her other arm. Her eyes felt groggy again, and she was unable to keep them open. They slid closed.

"Which are you giving her now?" a man growled from nearby.

"The cougar," a man answered from her other side. His raspy voice seeped down to her bones; wrapping around her and making her feel safe. A feeling she couldn't understand.

The what? Her mind raced to process the information. Her tongue felt too heavy and thick to ask.

"Where are the other vials?" Asshole One growled again.

"I moved them to a secure location. We don't want them tainted," silky-voiced Asshole Two answered.

"Make sure you give her all of them except the bear. Boris plans to bite her himself. He thinks the DNA in his saliva will work faster."

"That wasn't the plan," Asshole Two

was quick to say.

"The plan changed. Just do as you're told or you'll be joining her," Asshole One growled.

She heard his retreat and the click of the closing door. Her head lolled to the side because she was unable to hold it straight, and she moaned as the light dimmed, sucking her back into the dark void.

"Shit." Asshole Two whispered into her ear. "You're not supposed to be here. Fuck, you aren't even twenty-four yet."

She turned toward his voice, unable to open her eyes.

"Just hold on one more day, and I'll get you out of here." She felt his palm on her forehead and heard a low whistle like what she'd heard in the parking garage.

Darkness sucked her under, and all talking ceased. She never even saw the face of the man who promised to help her escape.

****

Pain radiated from her neck as a large body pressed down over her chest. Straps tore at her stomach and legs as she fought to get free. Her arms were strapped down by her sides. The only movement she had was in her fingers. She jerked at the confinement, and her eyes slid open. A large man was leaning down over her, his chest heavy on hers, his head buried deep in her neck. She screamed.

"Shut this bitch up," the man growled around his teeth which were lodged in her neck.

A hand covered her mouth, and she turned her head to see another man in a white lab coat. He stared back at her, pity in his eyes. He shook his head as if trying to still her.

"Don't move. It will only be worse."

Her whole body jerked, trying to dislodge the man's weight and his grip on her neck. She felt the tear of her skin, the ripping of her tendons, and an unbearable pain shot through her whole body as wet liquid ran down her neck. Bright white shot behind her eyes, leaving her gaze clouded and unfocused as tears slipped down her temples.

"Serves her right," the asshole growled, lifting up off of her. "I'll punish her for that when she's done turning. She needs to be taught a lesson."

"Boris," she heard Asshole Two yell as he entered the room. "Stop. You weren't scheduled to bite her until tomorrow. Are you trying to kill her?"

Her body grew weaker by the second. Her limbs went limp. She was dying. She knew it.

"Be mindful, boy," was Boris' only

answer. "Patch her up. If she dies, so do you."

Abigail welcomed the darkness this time as the pain engulfed her. She was ready for the numbing bliss. Her heart beat slowed as she waited for her death.

****

Voices faded in and out as feelings in her legs and arms started to return. Her eyelids still felt too heavy to open.

"You're going to kill her," a new voice announced as she felt another person at her neck. She felt the pull of the blood leaving her body as she slipped back into the darkness where time stood still.

Abigail pushed her way out of the gray haze toward the sound of the machine matching her heartbeat. Her weak body gained some strength as she fought to open her eyes. A palm rested on her forehead. An older man's face was her only view.

"You're a lucky girl, Abigail. We weren't sure you were going to make it. I'm Dr. Tanner."

Fear returned as memories surfaced of what Boris and the other assholes had done. Her gaze darted around the room as a scream bubbled to her throat.

"We're not going to hurt you. We're here to help you," Dr. Tanner announced, lifting his hands and stepping back. "This is Colton Trapp. He's the chief of SID, the Shifter Investigation Division."

"Where am I and how do you know my name?" Abigail shrieked while scurrying as far away as the IV's and machines would let her from the men. "What did you do to me?"

"An anonymous tip." The doctor answered with a frown while looking at the other man in the room before meeting her gaze again. "Whoever helped you escape left you in an alley, behind SID. You'd lost a significant amount of blood."

Abigail rubbed her wrists from where the restraints had scathed her skin. "I was abducted." A tear slipped down her cheek. "Those assholes..."

The man named Colton stepped forward and lifted a reassuring hand before dropping it back to his side. "Will die for what they've done."

She looked up into his eyes and knew he meant what he said.

"You'll kill them?" Her voice came out a whisper.

"They're killing innocent people. I'll do what's necessary, Abigail," he reassured her.

The skin on her arms tingled with a sensation she'd never felt before. She glanced down at her fingers. Her normally short nails were long and sharp. Orange and black hairs had started to sprout on her arms. Warmth radiated through her chest. Her heart raced, and her eyes widened as she held up her arms. "What did they do to me?"

"Take several deep breaths and fight your change. We need you coherent."

"What change?" Her voice rose an octave. "What are you talking about?"

"Calm down, and I'll explain."

Abigail took several deep breaths and closed her eyes, trying to will her heartbeat to slow down. She opened her eyes. These men weren't restraining her. She was safe.

"For as long as I've lived, there have always been people from opposite ends of the spectrum; they either hate shifters and want to destroy them or are looking for ways to be just like them. It's nature. Our intel suggests that the group that abducted you was trying to transform humans into shifters as a way to build an army. They've altered your DNA in an experiment to see if they could change you from human to shifter." He paused. "And they succeeded. We need your help to stop them from doing it to anyone else."

She looked down at her pale skin. Her voice was a whisper in the room. "They've ruined my life."

"Abigail," Colton said.

"Abigail's dead. Those bastards killed

her," she growled and lifted her gaze to meet Colton's. "And I'm going to return the favor, even if I die trying; you can count me in." *Starting with the man named Boris.*

Colton gave her a determined nod. "You aren't alone anymore, Abigail. I'm going to help you, train you, teach you, and turn you into their worst nightmare."

She pressed her lips together as hatred seeped into her bones, curling around every fiber of her being. They'd screwed up. They should have killed her while they had the chance. She wasn't weak anymore. She could feel the shimmering of the beasts stirring to life inside her body. They were just as thirsty for revenge as she was. She might not know how to control them yet, but she would. It was just a matter of time before she could return the pain they'd inflicted on her. The only difference was they wouldn't be saved, not from her. She slid her legs off the bed, trying to stand for the first time, and Colton stepped forward as if to catch her in the event she fell.

"Abigail, are you okay?"

Her eyes narrowed into slits. "I said Abigail is dead." She paused as the hot anger swept through her again. "Call me Elizabeth."

Chapter 2

Elizabeth Hanson tightened her grip on the silver shackles she'd attached to the killer's wrist. Any day another menacing shifter was taken off the streets was a good day in her book.

"And you thought you'd get away with the kill." She chuckled into Horace Stanton's ear.

The stupid wolf had been standing over the dead woman when she found him, like a winner claiming the prize. That sweet taste of victory he'd been enjoying had cost him. One paralyzing dart into his ass and he'd dropped to the ground like a ton of bricks. What a schmuck.

"Who the hell are you?" He leaned in, almost tripping over his feet to get close enough to get a deep breath near her neck. His look was priceless. "What the hell are you?"

He crinkled his nose and tried to yank from her grip. "I know one of those stenches." His lips curled up in a smile, giving her a glimpse of his blood-stained teeth. "You're one of Boris' bitches."

Not only his, but she kept that secret guarded close to her chest. The big bastard was hard to forget. He'd been the only one who'd demanded to use his teeth to infect her with his shifter DNA. One bite and she thought her world would end. One silver bullet to the head and his did.

Within days she'd tracked the other shifters that had kept her prisoner, shoving needles into her arm and injecting their unwanted DNA into her veins. The joke was on them. They'd taken the reason for abducting her to their grave. Well, most of them did. A couple had heard the rumors that she was coming for them and considered her a viable threat. The smart ones had gone into hiding, and it was just a matter of time before she found them, too.

Boris' savage mark and scent had faded over time, but the damage had already been done. Her future and happiness had been ripped from her in a matter of seconds. She would never have children and pass down her altered DNA, never have a mate, and never be human again. No matter how many shots the good Dr. Tanner gave her in an attempt to silence the beasts and return her to the normal life that she'd once lived. There would never be enough drugs to take her back.

The only plus side of the liquid shots he'd made, was that it altered the smell of the animals deep inside. The weekly medication was something she'd have to take for the rest of her life. If they'd known what she'd become, if anyone ever found out...she shivered at the thought. She was stuck between worlds, not a shifter, not a human, but something far more devious and deadly.

Colton Trapp had nursed her back to health and taken her under his wing. She'd turned her life around because of him. Her lust for blood was controlled; her only craving now was for justice against the breeds that had caused her hell.

Unluckily for the shifter in shackles, Hector's name had been next on her list.

"Hard to be someone's bitch when their sorry carcass is burning in hell, but try and pull away from me one more time, and I'll send you to join him."

Liz gave the shackles a hard shake and hurried the asshole down the long white sterile hall toward the empty holding cells. She ground her teeth to stave off any partial shift at the mention of Boris' name. Her blood heated and warmed beneath her skin, her teeth ready to strike. Which animal would emerge was the question she was unable to answer. She always guessed wrong. The grinding calmed her temper, even if she had to endure another lecture from her dentist. It was worth the scolding. She unlocked his cuffs and gave him a little push inside one of the empty silver cells. The click of the door locking into place produced a smile on her face.

"Enjoy your stay, asshole."

Horace wound his long fingers around the silver bars. Any other animal would have winced from the pain and retreated. Only the wolves were stupid enough to try. This guy was a douche. Of course, he tried. Pain etched his face, hardening his jaw. The stench of burning skin filled her nose, yet he hadn't flinched. He held on tight and deepened his hateful glare. He wouldn't be the first, or last, shifter that wanted to kill her. *Welcome to the club, asshole.* His eyes shifted from blue-green to the yellow of his animal and back again before he snarled.

"I'll be seeing you, detective." He gave a slow, calculating nod. "You can count on it."

Liz stepped closer to the bars, refusing to back down. 'Show no fear' was her only motto now. Didn't he know he was playing with fire? Stupid mutt.

She snaked her hand between the bars and gripped the shifter's neck, giving it a nice little squeeze. His eyes widened as he tried to peel back her fingers. Her ridiculous strength was thanks to the experiment. Her ability to control her temper was not. "Be careful what you wish for, wolf. I may look like an easy kill, but I can assure you, I'm not."

His face grew redder by the second, turning the shade of a ripe tomato in her old vegetable garden. His nails elongated, sliding out in a gamble to penetrate her skin.

"I'm not your prey." She spoke with venom in her voice. "You're mine." Her narrowing gaze turned everything red for a brief second, giving him a glimpse of her deadly dragon inside. Daggers stared back at her. Grinning, she shoved him, sending him flying into the back wall of the cage. His body collapsed to the floor as he rubbed his throat, gasping for air. The red marks around his neck, in the shape of her fingers, were already starting to fade.

"Hanson quit playing with the inmates." Colton Trapp's six-foot-seven body loomed at the end of the hall. His muscular arms crossed over his wide, big chest. She knew his beast. She'd witnessed his grizzly bear first hand. "In my office... now."

"This isn't over." The wolf's growl vibrated throughout the room as he eased off the floor, his claws sliding back into place.

"Suit yourself. It's your funeral." She whistled, leaving him to plot her demise, his measly threats cataloged with all of the other ones she'd accrued over time. Another one down. Her life might be a screwed-up mess, but damn, she loved her job.

The whistle died on her lips as she entered Trapp's office. He'd folded his big body into the leather chair, his look anything but bemused.

"I didn't hurt him," she blurted out while plopping down in one of the seats. "The moron threatened me, and I warned him against it. That's all I did. If you think about it, I did a good deed and saved his life."

Trapp leaned back in his chair with his elbows propped on the armrests. His steepled fingers and menacing stare had softened into a look of curiosity. He remained quiet as if watching and waiting for her to trip on her words. Criminals had cracked under pressure from his look. She wouldn't.

Her eyes locked on his, and her brow rose in question as she pressed her lips together. If it was a battle of the wills he wanted, she'd play that game.

Sweat beaded her brow the longer the silence lingered, every second tearing at her determination. The loud ticking of the clock hanging on the wall behind her mocked her. He was testing her resolve.

"Okay, fine. I may have issued my own threats back. But it was only in self-defense."

His lips twisted at the corners, giving her little reprieve.

He sat forward, folding his arms on his desk. "Do you remember when I found you?"

"Is that a trick question?"

"I picked you up, brushed you off, gave you a new identity, and I've seen to your medical treatment. Not to mention I gave you a job, somewhere constructive for you to steer your anger in a more productive way."

"And I appreciate that," she answered, mildly agitated that he would bring up the painful memories. "Your point?"

"It's time for you to return the favor. You're going undercover to work a case in the last place on earth you've sworn to never live."

Her eyes widened, and her heart quickened. Not the Glades, please don't say the Glades. She'd purposely stayed away from the Glades. The shifter community, an hour away, was the last place she'd ever feel at home. Aw, hell, the twinkle in his eyes told her that he was about to ruin her day.

"The Glades."

Like a knife shoved in through her heart, his confirmation was the final twist.

"There are dead bodies and missing people if it makes you feel any better."

She leaned forward, resting her elbows on her knees. Her foot tapped nervously on the ground. "Are you trying to get me to resign? All it's going to take is one of those assholes sniffing me and then it will be game on. One wrong word and it's not going to be pretty. You'll have a bloodbath on your hands and end up throwing my ass in jail for murder."

"You'll manage." He said it more as a direct order than anything else. He clearly believed in her self-control, more than she did.

Liz cleared her throat and straightened her shoulders. She could do this. She might not want to, but she'd survive and handle the challenge. She owed him, and this was one hell of a request. "What's the case?"

Trapp grinned for the first time since she'd walked into his office. He tossed a file to her side of the desk. "It's all in there. Your mission, your cover, everything you'll need." He gestured to the door with a tip of his head, dismissing her. "You'll be staying with *my* cousins. So play nice."

"Sir?" She tilted her head. "Won't that defeat the purpose of my cover?"

"No. They're the ones that noticed the similarities in the disappearances. Read the file, pack your things, and report in the morning. Unlike the morons that abducted you, this time it's both shifters and humans being abducted, and the common link so far is my cousins' bar, Liz. We need to find out who's behind it and stop them. Bring the fuckers to their knees. Do you understand me?" He pursed his lips. "Use any means necessary."

Oh, she understood all right. Where she was staying sucked and her assignment wasn't any better, but having full rein on her abilities was a bonus and an advantage. "Yes, sir."

KATE ALLENTON

Chapter 3

Elizabeth arrived home and dropped her bag onto the battered and scarred wood surface of her coffee table. Like everything in her home, once it had been new and beautiful and bright, but now it was tainted like her body and her mind. A few unexpected shifts into some big-ass scaly, motherfucking animals and she'd done the damage herself, so she couldn't really complain. She'd fought against the fire-breather's claim on her body, wishing like hell it had been one of the others that had surfaced instead. Even the wolf would have been better than the black dragon that singed the curtains with a simple sneeze. A wolf, lion, puma, bear, hell, she'd even been a dog and a cat when the doc had been trying to calculate the correct dosage of her meds. Her bones had contorted and twisted several times in an hour, before shifting into different forms, leaving her exhausted when it was all said and done. Which animal would appear next was anyone's guess. Owning nice things was a thing of the past. She made herself a glass of sweet tea and grabbed the confidential police file from her bag before dropping into the earthy brown plush recliner. She kicked up her feet, ready to get down and dirty in the details.

She dug into the file, a mystery to figure out. She read the entire thing, twice. Missing people was putting it mildly. The fliers for the missing, in the back of the folder, were all women ages twenty-one to thirty-five. They'd all gone missing in a five-block radius of the Honey Pot, the notorious human/shifter shared bar in the Glades, the only one in two hundred miles where it didn't matter what your species was. They'd take anyone's money in exchange for the liquor. The owners were either geniuses or daft. Humans were no match for shifters that held tempers. The security guard alone would have to be one hulking beast.

About half of the women reported missing were shifters, the other half humans, leading her to quickly rule out a hate crime. There were plenty who didn't like the idea of breathing the same air, and just as many more who didn't really care, not to mention the groupies begging to be turned, as though it was a damn privilege instead of a curse.

There were no leads, only the gender to go on. A chill skirted down her spine. She'd been a missing woman once, and the things they'd done to her.... She clenched her teeth to avoid the shift, trying to forget the horrendous memories. If the people responsible were playing the same game and had their hands in this mess, damn right, they'd pay. She'd see to it personally.

"You're wasting time, Hanson," she whispered, pushing the footrest back into place. "Another one could be snatched at any minute."

She grumbled as she headed into her room to pack her bag, making sure she had enough darts, knives, and guns to last her however long the mission was going to take. The darts she coveted were the ones they'd used to take down the biggest and worst shifters that the town of Crompton had ever seen. What she lacked in weapons, her animals would have to handle. Tossing some of her clothes, meds, and toiletries in the bag, she laid the file on top before zipping it up. A shower, another dose of the medication to mask her scent and she was out the door for her first look at the bar before any of the introductions were made.

Carrying her luggage to the front door, she gave one last, longing look around the apartment she was leaving behind. It wasn't much, but it was hers. She closed the door, not knowing when she'd be back. If she had her way, she'd have the case solved tonight.

****

Elizabeth relaxed in her car outside the Honey Pot. She could hear the beat of the music drifting out into the warm summer night air. The full, graveled parking lot brimmed with cars and trucks. For a Thursday night, the place was packed. She checked the ammo in the clip before shoving the gun into her leg holster and adjusting her jeans back into place. She'd opted to carry her SID badge clipped to her jeans, using the flowing material of her black shirt to keep it out of sight. One last swipe of lip gloss across her lips and she snatched the clutch from the passenger seat and stepped out of the car.

Various scents assaulted her nose, and she took a minute to decipher all of the animals nearby. The stench of musky wolves, the sweet and outdoorsy tinge of bears, and...she tilted her head and inhaled deeper, trying to determine the last smell... "What is that smell?"

Regardless of what they were, she straightened her shoulders, placed a fake smile on her face, and headed toward the doors. There were a handful of humans and shifters standing outside the door. Some were flirting, some talking, and others on the side of the building could have been charged with indecent exposure. A man had a woman pressed against the wall. Their grunts filled the air, along with the musky scent of sex. *It's just a bar, full of deadly animals, but still, just a bar,* she repeated in her head.

She stepped inside the building and paused as her gaze adjusted. The hypnotic music saturated her pores, tugging at memories she'd buried long ago. She wasn't here to enjoy herself. Hell, she couldn't remember the last time she had.

Scanning the occupants, she sized them all up, assigning a breed and the best way to beat them to a pulp, if the need arose. Several conversations had stopped as some of the men glanced her way. Gazes traveled from the red-painted toenails in her three-inch heels up to her face before the stupid ones dismissed her as a threat, returning to what they were doing. A few lust-filled gazes lingered, and she rolled her eyes. The magic drugs were working their mojo, hiding her scent.

"Excuse me." A dark-haired woman

with long, flowing hair stepped up next to Elizabeth and gave a genuine smile. "Here goes nothing." She wiggled her brows, pressing her palm to her stomach before sauntering toward a table in a darker corner of the club.

Elizabeth moved over to the bar and slid onto an empty stool. The six-foot-five grizzly pouring a beer from the tap glanced her way and winked. "Be with you in a minute, sweetheart."

The bartender's blue eyes twinkled with mischief as he handed the beer to an old man seated in front of the taps. The bartender's short brown hair was cut in military fashion. A flash of tattoos peeked out from beneath the sleeve of his shirt. There was no denying the relationship between this man and her boss. Their good looks alone confirmed that fact without her ever having to take a sniff.

He tossed the rag over his shoulder and headed in her direction. His black T-shirt stretched tightly across his broad, muscular chest. His jeans rode low on his tapered hips. She swallowed hard, trying her best to refrain from licking her lips. Getting involved with someone on an assignment wasn't an option. For her, it might never be.

"What can I get you?" he asked in a deep baritone voice that wrapped around her body, caressing it like a lost lover.

What the fuck was wrong with her?

"Just a bear."

Sex-on-a-stick shot her a sexy, devious smile, and she realized her mistake.

"I mean a beer," she amended and swallowed around the lump stuck in her throat. He made her nervous and antsy like nothing she'd ever felt.

He placed his palms on the bar and leaned forward as if peering into her soul. He inhaled and tilted his head, letting his baby blues caress her face, touching every inch of her down to her chest with his hungry gaze.

She clenched her legs together, fighting against his pull, against giving him any sign of interest. Her job was going to be hard enough without all of the dirty thoughts swimming through her head. Damn.

"You do have beer, don't you?" she prodded, trying her best not to use a come-hither voice.

His lips twisted into a full grin in response before he broke her gaze, giving her room to breathe. He pulled a bottle out of the cooler next to him. Flicking off the top, he set a napkin down in front of her before placing the bottle on top.

"You're new in town," he said more as a statement than a question, using the same tactic her boss was famous for.

Remembering why she'd been sent was

the only thing that made her hormones transform from an all-out frenzy to a dull simmer she could handle.

"Is that a question?" she asked, after taking a long pull of the ice-cold brew. The liquid cooling her throat helped ease the tension in her shoulders.

"No, I'd remember you." He held out his hand. "My name's Rhys."

"Lizzy." She gripped his hand, and his long fingers closed around hers. Instantly, tingles traveled from her palm up her arm and through her body, engulfing her in quick, consuming flames. Heat flooded her body, moisture pooling between her legs.

His brows dipped, his smile slipped, and he inhaled a deep breath. Confusion clouded his bright blue eyes before his gaze grew intense. His eyes deepened to a dark blue, swirling with a new zest. He blinked, and her mouth parted in shock.

Staring back at her wasn't the flirty bartender she'd just met but the bear beneath the skin. Crap. The thin restraints on his animal were barely held in check. The musky scent of his bear muddled the other scents in the room, surrounding her and pulling her further under his spell. The sounds of the music and conversations faded away as his gaze locked with hers. The heat of his fingers ignited a fire deep in her core, and the need to jump the counter, into his arms, to latch onto to his lips was almost unbearable. In that one second, they were alone; it was just him and her, with no threats of danger nearby. The word danger stuck in her mind, over and over in her head like a repeating song on her playlist. The repetition effectively broke through his spell, pulling her back to reality and the reason she was there. Getting laid was going to have to wait, no matter which of her animals was attempting to break free. She shoved that bitch back down beneath the surface and tightened the reins. No...she was there to do a damn job, and it didn't include a roll in the sack with the sexy bartender. SHIT.

She yanked her hand free, rubbing it on her jeans. Instantly, she surrounded herself in a protective bubble, the way one of her psychic coworkers had taught her so she could keep everyone out of her personal space.

"Lizzy." He murmured her name like a lover, testing the sound on his sensual lips.

Elizabeth squirmed on her seat to ease the throb between her legs.

He inhaled, and she hoped to hell he couldn't scent her arousal. His eyes flashed again. "Mine."

That answered her question.

"Hardly," she said in a measly attempt to beat the man and his beast back into submission. She wouldn't let him forget the reason she was there. The word meant to collar his reaction had the opposite effect. His nostrils flared before he stormed off in the opposite direction, leaving his post behind the bar. He rounded the corner, stomping over to where she sat, and his big leg brushed her legs apart to stand between her thighs. He rested his palm on her face, gently brushing his thumb across her lips. His tenderness caught her off guard, confusing her and ratcheting her own desires.

She shoved against his unmovable chest, trying to reclaim her personal space. He didn't budge. She bit her lip, trying to stave off calling up any of her animals for strength, but she damn sure would if she couldn't talk him off the ledge. The imaginary wall she'd created to keep him out popped like a bubble landing against thorns.

"You're crowding me." She grabbed his legs in a punishing grip, not pushing him away, thereby contradicting her words. She licked her lips, and he lowered his head. Her breath came out in quivering pants as she tried not to breathe in his heady musk.

"I'm Elizabeth Hanson." She blurted out her full name. Her name made him pause, giving her the reaction she might not have wanted but most definitely needed. "Your cousin sent me, and you're blowing my cover."

Her words were a whisper between them, while she used her job as a shield, like the badge secured to her waist that she flashed against criminals. No amount of heart-pounding, heat-searing, blood-pumping lust was worth another life hanging in the balance. Not even the big-ass bear standing between her thighs could deny what she said was the truth. Oh, he'd try, but he wouldn't succeed. The only way she'd succumb to instant gratification would be by killing the fuckers behind the abductions.

"This"—she gestured between them—"can't happen." She rested her palm against his large chest, trying to ease him back. Claiming heat seared beneath her palm. The wild animal wanted his mate.

"Rhys," another man called out from behind the counter. "Quit accosting the customers."

"Fuck off," Rhys growled back without even a glance toward the owner of the voice. He continued to loom over her, engulfing and consuming her. His gaze locked with hers. His heart thumped furiously against her palm. "Just so we're clear." His eyes swirled from baby blue to a dark gray storm and back. "This is happening. So wrap your pretty little mind around it."

"Little?"

His lips twitched seconds before he crushed them to hers in a claiming kiss. Against her better judgment, she parted in invitation, for once in her life, for a mere second, throwing caution into the wind. She let him past the walls that had kept her alive. He tilted his head, deepening the taste, stroking his tongue against hers. He was claiming her with his scent, with his mouth. She savored his taste and pulled him closer, eliciting a growl from deep in his chest. His hands tangled in her hair, and she was trapped. Visions of the straps she'd been confined with flashed in her mind and her pulse raced for an entirely different reason. She couldn't do this. No. She shoved against his chest and turned her head, breaking the connection as panic gripped her tight.

Rhys kept his hand on her leg, but she could read the mixture of emotions on his face. "Elizabeth."

She met his gaze, and heat flooded her body for an entirely different reason. The aggravation and agitation returned, putting her in the frame of mind she'd become accustomed to. "Not here." She shook her head.

"Rhys. We need more beer from the cooler." The voice of the person who'd called him before shouted even louder this time.

"We'll talk tonight."

With those words, he stepped back, giving her much-needed room to breathe. He stormed off toward the other end of the bar. Another brown-haired man was slinging beers behind the bar. He ran a hand through wavy hair that curled at his collar. The same high cheekbones and hard jaw left little doubt he was Rhys' brother. Elizabeth kept a critical eye, watching Rhys until he disappeared into a backroom. She grabbed some bills from her purse and left them under her beer before quickly sliding off the stool. One last glance around the bar and she hurried to the exit, not breathing again until she was behind the wheel of her car. Her resolve firmly in place, she pulled out of the parking lot, dust flying from the squeal of her tires, not giving Rhys a chance to chase her. She had one more night to herself before she had to report in for the job, and she was damned if she was staying under his roof.

Sliding her phone out of her purse, she dialed the familiar number and took a deep breath, trying to calm her heart and her mind.

"What?" Trapp growled into the phone.

"Sir...we have a problem."

Chapter 4

Trapp's deep belly laughter rang out through her cell phone's speaker, filling the silence in her car. The sound was foreign to her ears. She'd been expecting understanding, hell, anything other than humor at her expense. Elizabeth gripped the steering wheel tighter, turning her fingers white as anger boiled her blood. "Sir, this is not funny."

"Sure it is, Elizabeth." Trapp cleared his throat, trying to stifle his chuckle and failing miserably. "Welcome to the family." She could hear the smile in his voice. Damn man.

"He doesn't want me. He's attracted to the bear's DNA I was injected with, not mine."

"Oh, come on, Lizzy; you don't know that."

"Don't I? He thinks I'm his mate." Her voice rose in despair. "What the hell am I supposed to do now?"

"Abigail."

Hearing her given name made her pause. Trapp never used her real name. Heck, he'd helped her to erase any trace of the shell of the woman she'd been before the attack. That long-forgotten name, meant to grab her attention, worked.

"Any man would be happy to be your mate." The laughter from his voice disappeared. His tone turned gentle. She sighed.

"Don't call me that," she responded matter-of-factly with a slight chill in her voice. "Abigail Monroe is dead. Those bastards killed her."

"Abigail Monroe was a survivor; and no matter what you think about yourself and what those assholes did to you, you deserve to be happy. I'll be damned if I'm going to allow you to think you're any less of a woman because of those pricks. I don't give a shit what your name is or what animal you can shift into. I know the woman who works for me, and I wouldn't change a damn thing about her, whether you call yourself Abigail or Elizabeth. It doesn't fucking matter. What matters is that you survived, and they can't take that away from you."

If only that were true. "How do you want to me to handle Rhys?"

"He's a strong bear, Lizzy. If he believes you're his mate, there won't be any stopping him from pursuit. The fact you left the bar without saying a word is going to drive his bear insane. Not to mention the fact you still have a job to do."

Elizabeth pulled the car over onto the embankment and rested her head on the headrest. She closed her eyes, letting the knowledge she had to go back sink in. It was inevitable. She knew it, and he knew it. "I have no choice, do I, sir?"

"Afraid not, Elizabeth."

"I have to go back."

"Be upfront with him. Tell him the truth about what happened to you. Give him a chance to understand why you're scared."

"What? No! I'm not telling a stranger what the hell happened to me. I'll just have to convince him that he's wrong. I'm not the girl he wants. I'll never be a mate he'll be happy with."

Trapp held more confidence in her than she held in herself. Sharing her secret wasn't an option on the table. The embarrassment alone would kill her newfound confidence. She'd been treated like an animal, and no one had even noticed she'd been missing. Her life had been pathetic, and worse, it was still pathetic. The only thing that changed would be that at least Trapp would notice if she up and disappeared one day.

"Yeah, good luck with that." He chuckled again. "Listen, if it will help, I'll have a word with him and explain that you weren't born a shifter. That should at least slow him down. It will buy you some more time while you decide if you want to share the details."

"You'd do that for me?" she asked.

"Lizzy, I will always look out for you, not only as your boss, but as your friend. Now find a hotel and get some rest. You can go to their house in the morning. It will give him some time to calm down, and everything will look better in the light of day."

"Thanks, Colton," she said, ending the call. Time was something they both needed. She needed to figure out how to handle the big bad bear, and he...Well, he needed to figure out how he was going to keep his distance.

****

After thirty minutes of his cousin's constant calling, Colton Trapp shut his phone off and eased out of the bed, throwing on some clothes. An hour later, he stood outside his cousins' door. Colton rapped his knuckles against the wood. He heard the arguing inside. Shadows flicked across the window, blocking the light. A loud crash banged inside before he heard the wailing growl of one pissed-off bear.

The door flew open and Rhys, bare as the day he was born, pegged him with the glare, as he stood on the threshold. His electric-blue eyes swirled from blue to gray as though he was seconds away from ripping Colton's head off.

"Settle down, bear. I came to discuss your mate."

"Where is she?" Rhys growled while fisting his hands. Barely contained fury simmered just beneath his skin, threatening to break free. No wonder Elizabeth was scared. Rhys was acting like a lunatic.

Colton straightened his shoulders, waiting until Rhys regained control and his eye color flashed back to blue. "Good. Now as much as the ladies might enjoy seeing you in the buff, I don't. Go put on some damn clothes so we can discuss your situation."

Colton walked into the house, bumping Rhys' shoulder in passing. Rhys' brother, Max, glanced up with broken lamp pieces in his hand. "Took you long enough."

"Yeah, well, imagine my surprise

getting a call in the middle of the night from my best investigator explaining the problem."

"I don't know what name she's using, but she isn't booked at any of the local hotels under Elizabeth Hanson," Dylan announced while walking into the living room, looking down at the open phone book he carried in his hands. He glanced up, meeting Colton's gaze.

"You won't find her if she doesn't want to be found." Colton moved farther into the living room and waited until Rhys returned with his jeans up and zipped before continuing.

Dylan flicked the book closed and tossed it onto the coffee table. It landed with a loud thud. "Why the hell didn't you return our calls? You could have put the poor bastard out of his misery hours ago."

"I've been debating on my course of action." Colton gestured for them to have a seat.

Max plopped down in the recliner with his legs hanging over the side while Dylan relaxed on the couch. Rhys, the poor bastard, sat down on the oak coffee table, and the wood moaned from his weight.

Colton stepped to the fireplace and took a deep breath, figuring a way to tell them about Elizabeth without breaking her trust. "There are some things you need to understand about my investigator before I allow her to stay under this roof." He held Rhys' glare. "She wasn't born a shifter."

"Someone changed her?" Rhys rose from his spot, his eyes swirled dark gray; the muscles of his arms bunched, holding back the bear clinging beneath the surface.

"Yes," Colton confirmed. "Against her will, no less, but"—Colton held up his hands to stave off their questions—"make no mistake, he wasn't her mate, and she killed the assholes who hurt her. I was just the one who found her and helped her pick up the pieces of her life."

"Assholes? As in more than one!" Rhys took a step toward him before stopping.

"There are things you don't understand about her."

"That explains why she ran," Max said more to himself than anyone else. "She's scared."

"I'd never hurt my mate," Rhys growled, turning a deadly glare on his brother. "There's no reason to be afraid of me."

Colton paced the length of the living room. "Scared isn't quite a word I would use to describe Elizabeth." He glanced back at Rhys. "She's headstrong, bright, and competent just to name a few of her good qualities." He paused before continuing. "She's also got anger issues, and I hate to be the bearer of bad news, but she's not overly fond of shifters."

Rhys remained quiet. His brows dipped in confusion.

"She only trusts me because I earned it, and I'm afraid you're going to have to do the same."

"Exactly what has she been through?" Rhys prodded.

That was the only question that Colton wouldn't answer. "That's not my story to tell," Colton acknowledged apologetically. "I just came here to explain that she's just not used to being a shifter, much less our customs. The idea of a mate, and what it represents, is a foreign concept to her. So the minute you act like a caveman, she'll have you on your ass, unconscious in ten seconds flat, before she disappears out the door."

Colton stopped pacing. "She is...that good, that strong, and that cunning. I should know; I trained her. I expect all of you to show her some respect. She's here to do a damn job." He glanced at Rhys. "She won't care that you found your mate, especially if it derails her from the mission. So as hard as it's going to be, if you have any hope of mating with her, you're going to have to allow her some space and let her do her damn job."

"Fuck." Rhys stood and walked around the back of the couch. "You're asking me to be okay with putting my mate in harm's way."

"I'm not asking you. I'm giving you a piece of advice. If you even want a chance with her, you won't try and change her. She lives for the job. Throwing bad guys behind bars, especially if they're shifters, is the only way she's learned to cope and survive with what happened to her."

"What did happen?" Max asked.

Colton shook his head. "Sorry. I can't tell you, but let's just say it's ten times worse than you or I could ever imagine and leave it at that." He locked his gaze with the Rhys. "Don't fuck this up. She needs you as much as you need her, although she'd never admit it." He patted Rhys on the back and walked toward the door. "Good luck and keep me posted."

Chapter 5

Elizabeth pulled up at Rhys' large two-story home nestled in the middle of the one-hundred-acre property. Three bear shifters needed room to run. She understood that. Hell, she could even understand the size of the house, if both of Rhys' brothers were his size. Deep, rich red bricks covered the front of the house, white shutters framing each window. A large wooden porch wrapped around the front. Rocking chairs had been strategically placed for lounging. Rhys sat on the steps of the concrete porch with a coffee cup in his hand watching her with a predatory gaze, not making a move to approach the car.

She killed the ignition and popped her

trunk. His brow rose, and he gave her a lopsided grin as she stepped out of the car. Dew sat on the blades of grass in the early morning hours. Unable to sleep last night, she hadn't bothered waiting for the brothers to be awake. She'd planned to scope out the place, getting a feel for the lay of the land before they rolled out of bed. She inhaled a deep breath of fresh, crisp, clean air, heaving her bag out of the small trunk. She slammed it shut, coming face to face with Rhys. In the minute it took her to pull her bag out, Rhys had left the porch and stood by her side, and she'd never heard him coming.

"I thought bears were loud," she said, breaking the awkward silence.

"Only when trampling through the forest or chasing their mates." He grinned.

"Listen..."

Rhys took the bag from her hands and shook his head. "I'm sorry about last night. I wasn't expecting you. I mean...I was expecting Elizabeth, but I wasn't expecting to...oh never mind. Let's start over. I just want to get to know you, Elizabeth."

Elizabeth's mouth parted. His electric-blue eyes staring back at her were sincere. He tenderly brushed a strand of hair behind her ear. His eyes crinkled at the corners as he smiled. She would have swooned just from his touch if she wasn't trying her best to keep her hormones in check.

"You talked to Trapp."

Rhys placed his hand on the small of her back, leading her up the porch. Heat from his mere touch pooled in her belly. "I did."

"Is that the reason for the nice-guy routine?"

Rhys opened the door and ushered her inside. "I'm always a nice guy. Don't worry. He wouldn't tell us your secrets." He grinned.

The house was huge, even larger on the inside. A brick fireplace was nestled in one of the walls with throw rugs in front. The wide furniture in the living room was lush and inviting. Lord forbid, she lay down to take a nap. She'd never get up. The smell of honey drifted in the air, tugging her lips into a smile. Three bears reminded her of the fairytale, although the three large men in the room looked nothing like the cuddly little suckers in her book. The other bartender from last night stood patiently waiting with another man she'd never seen before.

"Elizabeth, I'd like you to meet Max and Dylan." Rhys gestured to each. "Guys, this is Elizabeth."

"Welcome. Make yourself at home." Max's green eyes sparkled with mischief. Right or wrong, she immediately labeled him the instigator of the bunch.

"Thanks." She smiled back. "Hopefully, this case won't take too long to solve, and then I'll be out of your hair."

Max's and Dylan's eyes widened, and their gazes shot to Rhys. His warm palm rested easily against her back. To his credit, he didn't growl, he didn't argue, he didn't fight. Maybe he'd been sincere.

"Rhys, why don't you show Elizabeth her room while we finish making breakfast?" Dylan nodded back toward the kitchen. And now she knew who the mother hen of the clan was; either that or the big bad bear was just starved.

Elizabeth followed behind Rhys up the stairs and onto the landing. The open space branched out in two different directions, and it wasn't until this point that she realized she wasn't just standing in a two-story house but something more like a freakin' mansion.

"That's Max's wing." He pointed off toward the right. "He pretty much stays to himself, so you don't have to worry about him bothering you." He gave her another lopsided grin before gesturing back to the bottom level below. "Dylan's wing is on the main floor." He gestured toward the hallway on the left. "This is ours."

"You mean yours," she corrected him.

"Ours." His brows dipped as he continued to speak, ignoring what she'd said. "You'll have your own room next door to where I'll be staying." He ushered her farther down the hall and glanced down sideways at her. "It's a compromise. If you aren't sleeping with me, at least I'll be nearby."

She stifled her grin. Rhys wasn't being very subtle about what he wanted, but at least he was trying. "My own room will be perfect, thank you."

He shoved open one of the doors and stood on the threshold waiting as she stepped into the extra-large room and turned slowly in place. The place was huge, just like everything in the house. The double doors to the bathroom stood open wide, and she could see a spa inside next to the large shower. "This room is bigger than my entire apartment. You guys don't do small, do you?"

Rhys chuckled. The sound teased her ears, making her animals giddy with delight. "Darling, there's nothing small within these walls."

Her cheeks heated while she tried her best to ignore his sexual innuendo. Her curiosity peaked, she strolled over to the walk-in closet and noticed men's garments hanging on one side and the other side holding empty hangers. She spun to face him.

"This is your room?"

He gave a slight nod. "And that's my

bed." He set her suitcase on top of the mattress. "You might not be ready for me, but I've waited my whole life for you. I want you in my bed even if I'm not sharing it with you."

Her animals' ears perked at his proclamation. She chewed her lip, letting his words sink in. The woman might be leery, but it appeared her animals were ready and willing to extend an invite for him to stay. She gave one more glance toward the bed, her mind imagining his big, sexy body beneath the dark blue comforter and cotton sheets. What would it be like for him to sleep with her? Holding her and wanting her like she'd never been wanted before. She licked her lips at the thought before slowly pushing the images to the back of her mind. It would be easy to give in to him, to let him ravish her and sate her until she was begging for more. Maybe, one day, when she wasn't worried about the damage one of her animals might cause. No, she couldn't let that happen. She wouldn't risk the possibility of losing the tight reins she held the beast with. Hurting him wasn't an option if one tried to make an unexpected appearance.

He stepped up behind her, pressing his chest to her back. His hands rested gently on her waist. "I can't promise to keep my hands off of you while you're here," he whispered into her ear, "but I can promise that I won't climb into that big bed without an invitation."

"This is a bad idea. Maybe I should go back to the hotel."

He lowered his head and inhaled a deep breath before he dropped his hold and stepped back, taking with him the warmth of his body. "That's not necessary, especially when you have three men willing to help you solve your case." She heard the disappointment in his voice and saw it in the shadows that flickered in his eyes. "Come on. Let's eat."

****

Rhys inhaled a deep breath, taking in Elizabeth's familiar scent and letting it wrap around his body. His cock hardened against his zipper, and it took every bit of control he had to drop his hands and step away when all he really wanted to do was bend her over the nearest chair and bury himself deep inside of her hot channel until she screamed his name in ecstasy. How the hell was he supposed to do "slow" with her? Her unusual, intoxicating smell made him drunk with need. She smelled of sweet honey with an exotic spice that he couldn't name. If she was a bear, he couldn't tell what kind. Hell, he didn't care. She was his, and he was hers, no matter if she was too stubborn to acknowledge it.

Unable to stop himself from touching her again, he slid his fingers through hers and guided her back down the hall, pointing out the room next door where he'd be sleeping. A single wall would be separating them tonight. He'd take what he could get until she decided to give in to the lust that was evidently tugging beneath their skin. It was like a live wire. He could feel it every time he touched her, and he'd lay money that she could feel it, too.

She didn't pull free, even though her body stiffened, uncertainty on her face. A small victory for him as the underlying storm brewed within her. *Get ready for me, doll.* He grinned to himself, released her fingers, and jogged down the stairs ahead of her.

"Food and then work?" he asked while walking backward through the living room. He couldn't take his eyes off her, not after she'd run last night and he didn't know if he'd ever see her again. No, he wouldn't be letting her out of his sight. Not now, not until he convinced her that they were meant to be together.

"I appreciate your hospitality." She slowed, stopping a foot away from him. "But let's deal with the elephant in the room. What's it going to take for you to realize I'm not your mate and this can't happen?"

Keep lying to yourself, sweetheart.

"How does this work? A quick roll in the sack, a bite of my neck?"

Hell yeah, now she's talking.

She crossed her arms over her chest as if she'd read his mind. The body language meant to close him off did nothing more than lift her perky breasts for a better view.

Damn, she was feisty. His bear growled with desire and approval. "First of all, when I take you to bed, it will be anything but quick. I'll spend hours tasting and worshiping your body." His lips quirked in an attempt to hold in his grin. "The biting can happen at any time, but it generally happens when I have you in a lust-filled haze, when you can't think of anyone or anything other than what it feels like to have me thrusting inside you." He said it matter-of-factly. "You'll accept me as your mate, the one man who can please you unlike any other, and I'll accept you as the one woman that I'll love for the rest of my life. Some shifters look at it as an age-old tradition that tells all of the other shifters to back the hell off. But with me...it's so much more. You'll be mine, and I'll be yours."

He closed the distance between them and cupped her face. "As for you being my mate, I don't need a bite to tell me you are. I already know it. One taste from your lips,"—he felt the shimmer of his beast trying to surface—"the electricity from your touch, the way you look at me..." He swiped the pad of his thumb across her juicy red lips, dying to continue the kiss he'd started last night. "Your scent may have peaked my interest, but your kiss fueled my flame. Make no mistake, Elizabeth Hanson, you *are* mine, and I *am* yours."

Her expression turned guarded at the mention of her name. She took a hesitant step back instead of leaning into the warmth he offered. He'd had her. For a brief second, he saw the resignation in her eyes and electricity stirring between them. The mention of her name worked like scissors cutting the cord.

"Thanks for the lesson, but I think I'll pass." She sidestepped around him disappearing into the kitchen. His bear roared in aggravation. The animal wanted her just as much as the man, equally wanting to haul her over his shoulder and take her back upstairs and kiss her until she admitted he was right. She was going to be the death of him. His self-control was being tested. "Damn."

The house phone rang as he stepped into the kitchen. Elizabeth was already seated and involved in easy banter with his brothers. The lucky assholes. How could she be so at ease with them after just meeting them, instead of with him after their shared kiss?

"Speak," Rhys barked into the phone while watching his mate interact with his brothers. She took a small bite of the bacon and grinned, and his heart melted more by the second.

"Put Elizabeth on the phone." Trapp's voice was anything but cordial.

"Lizzy." Rhys held out the phone. "It's the warden."

Elizabeth brushed his fingers while taking the phone from his hand. The small contact made her frown, yet made him grin. "Hello."

Her brows dipped lower with each second that passed. She was quiet, listening rather than talking. She nodded a few times. "Yeah, he's standing right here." She glanced up at Rhys. "Yeah, we'll be right there."

She shoved the phone into his chest and shrugged. "Time for work, fellas. It appears you guys are coming with me."

She grabbed another piece of bacon before disappearing out of the kitchen.

"Trapp, she just got here. Can't this wait?"

"Afraid it can't. They found another dead body, and the marks on her body, indicate this one was killed by a shifter."

There was a slight pause. "She was found less than a mile away from the club, with one of your matchbooks sitting next to her hand. We need you guys to come with Lizzie to see if you can identify her."

"Even if we don't, we can check the surveillance at the club. If she was there, we'll know who she left with. We'll be there in fifteen minutes."

Rhys hung up the phone, informing his brothers what he'd been told. They were on their feet and all of them out the door in mere minutes.

Chapter 6

Rhys opened the passenger door of the SUV and held out his hand.

How old does he think I am....five?

She shook her head and slid out without his assistance. The crime scene unit from the shifter division was already on-site, combing the alleyway and dropping numbered cones where potential evidence lay on the street. A blue sheet covered the dead woman's lifeless body.

"What do we know?" she asked, walking toward Trapp. Rhys and his brothers followed silently on her heels. She heard their deep inhale while sniffing the area. She rolled her eyes.

"Human female, Caucasian, left nude, out in the open for anyone to find. No identification or personal belongings," Trapp answered. "Matchbook from the club found next to her hand." He pointed toward the ground where it lay covered in blood. "I'm not even positive she'd been there."

She crouched, lifting the sheet. A woman's pale, lifeless face lay turned toward the side, her green eyes opened wide and unfocused. Her mouth gaped as if she'd been killed in mid-scream. Her dark brown hair was matted with the blood flowing from beneath her body. Elizabeth recognized her immediately as the woman who'd walked into the club behind her. She'd been nervous when she'd whispered, 'Here goes nothing.'

"She was there last night. She arrived the same time I did." Elizabeth replaced the sheet and stood. "I smelled her fear before she walked off toward the table in the northwest corner of the club. The corner was dark." She glanced up at Trapp. "She mumbled, 'Here goes nothing,' as she walked away."

Rhys pulled back the sheet so his brothers and he could get a better look at her face.

"Emily." Max breathed out her name; his voice stung with sadness. "Poor girl. She was a human groupie who wanted to be turned." He kept gazing down to the sheet, and remorse filled his eyes "About a month ago, she begged me to bite her, and I told her no."

Elizabeth bent down again and peeked beneath the rest of the sheet at the wounds covering Emily's body. Deep slash marks, torn down to the bone, covered the pale skin on her chest and down the length of her torso. Flesh and tendons were torn from her neck, and there were more teeth marks further up her neck where the fucker had bitten her. The asshole responsible was an aggressive shit. An odd sensation of déjà vu skirted down her spine, and goose bumps rose on her arms. The markings were similar to the previous homicide she'd worked, the same crisscross design left on the last dead woman, compliments of the wolf Elizabeth had locked away in a cell.

"Do you think this is an attempted turn gone wrong?" Rhys asked.

"Nope, this was violent," Elizabeth answered. "He might have lured her away with promises of turning her or even having sex, but the asshole tore out her throat and left his marks all over her body." She tilted her head and crossed her arms over her chest. Taking a deep breath confirmed her suspicions, the smells were similar; she continued, "Sir." She glanced up to find Tripp watching her. "It's an identical kill to the one I arrested Horace Stanton for. You'll need to put a rush into the lab to compare both kills against his DNA. Horace may have been standing over her body, but this kill happened after he was behind bars. I arrested the wrong guy. Either way, the lab will be able to confirm from the DNA."

"Elizabeth." Trapp's jaw clenched. The powerful force of his energy rolled over her.

Rhys stepped to her side. The heat from his big, brooding body warmed and surrounded her in a silent show of support without even a single touch.

"You know what the smug bastard threatened to do when he's released?"

She clasped her hands in front of her. "Yes, sir. He'll come after me and give me a whole new set of charges to arrest him for."

"Don't sugarcoat his threats, Elizabeth. He threatened to kill you," Trapp amended, most likely to clue Rhys in on the situation. Could he have made her look any more incompetent for arresting the wrong guy? *Jerk.* Thanks to him, her overprotective bear would be breathing over her shoulder for the entire investigation.

"He won't touch her," Rhys growled, and his brothers stepped closer, flanking them both.

"Get a grip. He can try, but we both know he won't succeed," she retorted before dropping the subject and heading back over to the SUV. She opened the passenger door and turned to find the men standing where she'd left them. "Don't we have some surveillance to look through so we can catch this guy?" she challenged with a lift of her brow.

****

Elizabeth stepped into the security room of the bar, expecting to find a small dinky room with bad lighting, and even worse, smaller computer screens, but she was wrong. The room was filled with long conference tables and large computer screens. A locked cabinet rested along the length of the back wall. She sniffed. Gunpowder, and from the size of the cabinet, she would have thought these guys were ready for WWIII.

A fridge was pressed up against the wall with a long counter running beside it. A full coffee station and espresso machine perched on top. Toward the back of the room, another conference table sat. The room reminded her of a typical office lunch room, combined with a conference room featuring full-on amenities.

"Nice setup."

"Glad you approve." Rhys rubbed

against her arm in passing before he clicked on the computers, bringing images to life. She moved around the table with the others and watched as every room in the empty club lit up on the screens.

"This should be a walk in the park," she mumbled before hopping up to sit on top of one of the long conference tables, watching Rhys pull up last night's feed.

"Go back to ten-thirty, and you'll see her walk in behind me, talk to me for a second, and head off toward the table."

"Ten fifty-three," Rhys corrected. "I know what time you arrived. I already reviewed the footage to see if it would help me pinpoint where the hell to find you." His fingers flew over the keyboard before he stilled the shot of Elizabeth entering the club. A quick glance over his shoulder and he grinned as he tapped the play button. He pointed out Emily and switched screens for a better shot of more than just the door. They silently watched the woman saunter through the crowded room toward the darkened corner.

"You need better lighting in that corner," Trapp pointed out.

"There is a light in that corner. It must have blown," Max answered, rubbing his five o'clock shadow as he moved to stand by Elizabeth.

"It was probably tampered with," Elizabeth chimed in.

With the camera taking in the whole room, Elizabeth's eyes were glued to the images of Emily leaving the table with three of her girlfriends in tow. She turned down the same hallway as the bathrooms and the security office.

"Looks like a bathroom break," Dylan suggested and glanced at her. "Why do you girls go in pairs?"

She grinned. "So we can talk shit about the men at the table."

They fast-forwarded to see if they'd been followed down the hall or if they'd come out of the hallway.

Within ten minutes, they all walked back out and straight through the club toward the front doors. "Do you recognize her friends?"

"Yeah, they meet up at the bar about once a week," Rhys answered.

"Sadie, Marie, and Jennifer," Dylan supplied.

"Are they shifters?" she asked.

"Yes." Rhys glanced up at her.

"If she's friends with shifters, why was she begging everyone to convert her? Why couldn't they just do it?"

Colton cleared his throat and stepped to her side. "The ability to change someone from human into a shifter is passed down only through male DNA. It was intended as a way to ensure that any male shifter could change his mate, assuming the female was strong enough to endure the enzymes. It's not uncommon for a female to die trying if she's too frail or sick to handle that particular strand of the DNA code."

She spun on him accusingly. "How come you never told me that?"

"Because it didn't matter," he answered. Colton glanced at the others. "Do you really want to discuss that here? Now?"

That was one conversation they would be having, just not in present company. If females could die from the DNA, those bastards had been trying to kill her using not one male's DNA but several. Her anger returned, coursing through her veins as if her abduction had just happened yesterday. If she could kill them all again, she damn sure would. Elizabeth felt the raging heat rising through her body. Her gums ached as her sharp teeth tried to press through.

"Elizabeth, your eyes," Colton said.

She took a long, deep breath and started grinding her teeth in an attempt to calm herself. Rhys pressed a palm on her arm. "Lizzie?"

Her anger dissipated with his touch, simmering to a controllable point. He calmed her beasts into submission, making them purr with giddiness that he was near. Should she be grateful or pissed? She pressed her lips together and turned back to the monitor. Rhys gave a slight nod before releasing her. He spun in his seat, reaching for the button to shut down the video, but Elizabeth stopped him. She pointed toward the darkened corner. "There. Look, that guy is following them out. Do you know who he is?"

"Evan Stone," Max answered.

Evan moved around the crowded tables heading for the door before he paused and glanced directly toward the camera. He flashed a smug smile with a predatory gaze. Lifting his arm, he tapped on the face of his watch before disappearing out the front door.

"What the—"

Elizabeth cut off Max's question as she hopped off the table and turned to address the men in the room, taking charge in the only way she knew how.

"We need names and addresses for all of the other women." She glanced at Colton. "I'll pick up Evan and bring him in for questioning."

Rhys rose slowly from his seat. His eyes flashed with protest as he stalked closer toward her. "Like hell."

Her eyes narrowed and locked onto his gaze. She wouldn't be backing down. She had a damn job to do, even if it meant staying the hell away from the big bad bear.

"Rhys." Colton's voice rang in her ears, but her gaze held steady.

As if Rhys sensed her determination, knowing he wouldn't win this battle, he took a deep, calming breath. "That came out wrong." He glanced over her shoulder toward the others before returning to her gaze. "What I meant to say was, wouldn't it be better if you talked to the other women? They might be more receptive to opening up with you because you're a woman."

"He's right." To her chagrin, Colton agreed. "I'll take a team and pick up Evan while you go get statements."

Elizabeth tossed her hands up before using her shoulder to push through the group, only to be stopped by Colton's palm on her arm.

"Establish contact and get statements." His jaw ticked. "I expect you to go in armed. We don't know what we're up against, and I don't want you ambushed. Let's just hope all of her friends didn't fall victim to the recent abductions."

She nodded and headed toward the door, only to remember at the last second that she hadn't driven herself. "I'm going to need my car."

Rhys glanced at his brothers, and some type of silent communication transpired between the men. Both men gave a curt nod. "We'll take you."

"Listen here, buddy. I just need my car." She stepped up to Rhys. "I don't need a babysitter. I've survived my entire life without you or your brothers assisting me."

Rhys cleared his throat and held her gaze. "Gentleman, could we have a moment?"

"Rhys." She could hear the warning in Colton's tone.

Rhys glanced up. "I need a minute with my mate. I just want to talk to her."

"*She* is right here." She glanced over her shoulder to the others. "And just so you know, if you hear him screaming like a little girl...he deserved it."

"Come on, guys; let's give them a minute." Colton ushered the other two cousins out of the room.

Elizabeth laced her fingers together, waiting patiently for the others to clear out of the room. Rhys wanted to talk? She had plenty to say.

"Rhys—"

He held up his hand and moved to the other side of the table, out of her reach. Smart, not that a table would stop her from reaching him to strangle the life out of his very thick neck, but whatever made the shifter feel safe. "I understand your need to put criminals away, and I understand your need to be independent, and I respect that about you. I have no intention of standing in your way."

"Good."

He cleared his throat. "I just need you to understand something about me. Lizzie, I just found you, baby. When you ran out of the bar last night, my bear and I went out of our minds. I don't expect to be your constant shadow, but for right now...in these first few weeks, my bear and I need to be close to you. Not because we don't think you can do your job, but because the need to protect you is ingrained in both of us...the man and the beast. We just want to be with you. So please, just this once...humor me. I conceded on the sleeping arrangements; I'm not pushing you into a mating bond, and I won't interfere in the investigation, but let me be near you. I *NEED* to be near you."

His admission was sincere. She read it in his eyes, heard it in his words, and smelled his genuine concern. Over the last year, whenever she'd met a family member of a missing person, they all gave off the same worried scent. Elizabeth chewed her bottom lip between her teeth while weighing his request. It wasn't uncommon for shifter males to be possessive. It was in their nature. She knew that much for certain. She could even appreciate the fact Rhys wasn't trying to elbow his way into the situation through his association with

Colton, or act like a caveman and insist, as if that would've helped, but what did it mean if she acquiesced? That she was agreeing that they were meant to be mates? Was that something she was willing to do?

"You're thinking too hard," he announced. "How about we try the first girl, and if you don't like how it goes, we'll get your car."

She let out a deep breath and gave a quick nod. "Fine."

Chapter 7

What else could she SAY? *No*, he couldn't tag along? She was staying at his house, not to mention he was related to the one man who'd helped her when she needed it the most. She could give Rhys an inch and worst case, he screwed up, at least then she'd have a good reason to kick his butt to the curb.

A quick phone call to the station with the ladies' full names, thanks to their bar tabs, and she had all of the women's addresses.

Rhys pulled up outside of Emily's townhouse and killed the ignition. She hated to be the bearer of bad news, but it was all part of the job. She tilted her head, watching a man carry cardboard boxes out of Emily's home. His lips moved while he mumbled to himself. He hefted one of the boxes and tossed it into the bed of a truck before disappearing back inside the condo and out of sight.

Stepping out of the car, she unhooked the badge attached to her waist. She held it up, flashing it at the same man carrying another box out of the door. She sniffed the air, expecting nothing but the scent of a human. Admittedly, she was caught off guard smelling the cougar's scent coming from the shifter.

"Shifter Investigation Division, I'd like to ask you some questions."

The man's face remained blank while tossing the box into the back of the truck. "SID? What can I do for you?"

In general, cougars were a laid-back bunch unless someone was trying to take something they considered theirs. This guy was emitting a sweaty stench she knew all too well. It wasn't from hefting the boxes. These assholes were strong. It was the smell of fear. The ungodly odor smelled like hot tar being paved in hundred-degree weather on a sunny day. His eyes darted from hers to Rhys and his brothers who were standing behind her, all of them patiently waiting and watching his reaction.

"Can we take this inside?" She gestured toward the open door.

He chewed his lip, and his eyes shifted toward the green forest beyond the apartments.

"Don't do it." She raised a challenging brow. "A cougar's top speed is around fifty miles per hour. You won't win. Trust me; I'm faster."

It took him only five seconds and one deep breath before he gave up on the idea of taking off. "Come on. Let's get this over with."

All four of them followed the cougar back into the townhouse. Her eyes darted around the apartment, taking in all the feminine attributes, the pictures on the wall, the color-coordinated throw rug and matching couch pillows.

"What's your name?" she asked.

"Martin Shuman," he answered crossing his arms over his chest and keeping his gaze on the men with her. Stupid cat. Didn't he know she was the most deadly in their group?

"Well, Martin..." She glanced around at some of the boxes piled around the house. "We came to ask you some questions about Emily Fisher. Is she your girlfriend?"

"That two-bit whore?" he spat out.

"From the looks of things, I guess you had a rocky relationship?"

He dropped his fisted hands to his sides. "I told her the next time she didn't come home I was leaving....and I meant it."

She gave a slow nod, and from the corner of her eye, she followed Rhys circling around the living room as if looking for clues.

"She didn't have a choice about coming home last night."

"I doubt that," he spat out.

"I'm sorry to have to tell you like this, but she was murdered."

His mouth parted, and all of the anger and fight he'd been putting out released from his shoulders. "Murdered?"

"Afraid so." She studied him and his reaction. The shock on his face told her what she needed to know. He didn't do it. Unwilling to trust her instincts, she persisted with the same line of questions she'd ask everyone involved. "Do you have an alibi for last night?"

Rhys picked up a picture frame from the mantel and appeared to be studying the picture.

"Yeah, I worked until eleven and then went to a bar around the corner from the depot with a few of the guys. I didn't get home until around twelve thirty."

"Where do you work?"

"Mass transit," he answered. "The cameras on the busses can confirm my alibi."

She made a mental note to check.

"Where did she work?"

"Kleinfield and Summers," he answered while glancing over his shoulder to see what Rhys was getting into.

"An attorney?"

"Yeah." He turned to face her. "She called me around nine last night and said she was just leaving to go meet the girls at the Honey Pot."

"Why was she working so late? I thought attorneys kept banker hours."

"Because it was the only time that the prick, Senator Hayes, could fit her into his schedule."

Max stepped up by her side. "She was representing the asshole that wants all shifters to be microchipped?"

"From what I could tell, they weren't helping him with that. It was something else, but she never told me what."

Rhys set the picture down and glanced in her direction as if the conversation had just turned interesting.

"When was the last time you saw or talked to Emily?"

"We had lunch together. I told her I was working late, and she mentioned her meeting with the senator and that she was going to go have drinks with the girls at the Honey Pot."

"You called her a whore. Was she sleeping around?"

"I caught her cheating once before. She

begged me to stay, said that she'd only done it so we could be together. She wanted to be a shifter, and I wouldn't change her."

"If you knew she was desperate to be changed and willing to seek it from other men, why didn't you just bite her yourself?"

"Detective..." He glanced back over his shoulder toward Rhys before meeting her gaze again. "She wasn't my mate. We only get one turn for our mates, and I wasn't about to waste it on her. We had an easy relationship. I'd told her going into it that, if I found my mate, I'd be leaving her. She knew that from the beginning."

This was more information that no one had bothered to share with her. If what he'd said was true, then what did it mean that all of those different breeds of shifters had experimented on her and injected their DNA into her veins? Had they lost their rights to turn their mates or did it only matter if teeth were involved? Was it possible they were looking for a way around the one-turn rule?

Rhys rounded the coffee table, moving to her side. He pressed his palm to the small of her back, pulling her from her thoughts.

"I'm going to need the name of the man she cheated on you with and where I can find him."

"Bert Handcock, and as for where you can find him, he's buried six feet under at the local cemetery."

"Did you kill him?"

"Hell no, I wasn't going to jail for killing that sniveling little shit. Rumor has it he was killed because he didn't pay his gambling debts."

"One more question, Martin. Where can we contact you if we have any more questions?"

"I'm staying with my brother on the west side of town. My supervisor has my new contact information," he answered before collapsing on the couch.

Patrol lights glinted through the curtains. "The forensic team is here to go through her things. We appreciate your time, and I'm sorry for your loss." She gave him a curt nod before ushering Rhys and his brothers out of the house and leaving the door open for the incoming team and detectives. Rhys and his brothers slid into the SUV, while she stopped, exchanging words with the lead assigned to search the house. She'd explained why Martin had some things packed and asked for the investigator to call her should they find anything out of the ordinary.

Martin stepped out of the house as she finished her conversation. "Hey, Detective..."

"Yeah?"

"I hope you nail this son of a bitch. Emily and I may have had our problems, but she didn't deserve to die, not for just wanting to be different."

"No...she didn't," Elizabeth mumbled beneath her breath while sliding into the front passenger seat. She pulled out her phone and started making notes as a reminder to check his alibi and Emily's work. They were getting nowhere fast, and she wondered if Trapp was having better luck on his end.

"Where to next?" Rhys asked, turning the key in the ignition.

"2710 State. Let's start with Sadie Miller."

Ten minutes later, they pulled up outside a well-kept small house on the east side of town in one of the older neighborhoods. An elderly lady stood with her body out of sight, peering from behind sheer curtains. Elizabeth stepped out of the SUV and held the door open, leaning back inside. There was something about this lady. Maybe it was the way she didn't want to be seen or the fact that she'd been watching the street for a reason. Was it because she knew more? Call it gut instinct or intuition. Either way, the boys needed to stand down on this one, or they might run the risk of the woman not talking at all.

"You guys should stay here. The old lady peeking out the window looks kind of spooked, and you three together might give her a heart attack before I even get to ask any questions." She smiled. "Isn't that why you said I should be talking to the women in the first place?"

Elizabeth chuckled and slammed the door. A whistle slid from her lips while she walked up the sidewalk to the door. She didn't even have to knock before it was jerked open and she came up close and personal with the barrel end of a shotgun pointed at her chest.

"Not another step," Granny growled.

"Shifter Investigation Division. I need to speak with Sadie."

Elizabeth heard the SUV doors open, and she glanced behind her narrowing her eyes, challenging them to make another move. Giving a little shake of her head, she turned back around, greeting the old woman with a smile on her lips.

"What's this about?" she asked and lowered the gun.

"I just have a few questions for her about one of her friends."

"Granny." A five-year-old child stepped into view, holding a baseball and a glove. "I'm going to practice catching."

He glanced up at Elizabeth with big brown eyes and smiled. "Who are you?"

Elizabeth leaned down and smiled.

"My name is Lizzie. I'm just a friend of your Granny and stopped by to talk to her for a few minutes." Elizabeth glanced behind her toward the truck, and she grinned. "I bet my three partners would love to play catch with you. Why don't you go ask?"

The little boy's eyes widened, and he glanced up at his grandmother. "Can I go play with the bears?"

"Wait. How did you know what they are?"

The boy placed his palm on her shoulder. "I can see them both ways. My daddy said it was a special gift from him to me."

"What do you see when you look at me?" she asked, tilting her head, ignoring the old lady and focusing her attention on the child.

"A whole bunch of animals, like at the zoo." He took her hand and closed his eyes. "Your daddy gave you a gift."

"Sorry, boo, but my daddy wasn't a shifter. Are you sure it wasn't bad men you see?" she asked, thinking maybe the kid had seen what they did to her with the DNA.

"Your daddy was special, like king of the jungle."

King, huh? She hadn't turned into a lion yet, but she guessed anything was possible.

He grinned. "Your momma was, too." He studied her and lifted a finger to cover her lips. "Shh, it's a secret."

"What is? I'm good at keeping secrets. You can tell me," Elizabeth said, not sure what to think of the kid's abilities. Her parents weren't special. They'd been human. She hadn't been changed until she'd been abducted. This kid had to be seeing the bad men and was mistaken when he mentioned a woman. From what she'd recently learned, women couldn't pass down the DNA, and she'd not seen any during her captor's experiments.

He leaned toward her and whispered into her ear. "She could disappear. I bet she was hard to play hide and seek with."

Okay...this kid definitely had an active imagination.

Elizabeth pretended to lock her lips and throw away the key.

She winked at him and ruffled his hair. "Why don't you go play with the bears? They're big, but I promise they don't bite."

Elizabeth glanced up at the old woman. "Is that okay, Granny? They'll stay in the yard where you can see him."

"Sure," she answered, and they both watched the child run toward the SUV.

Rhys rolled down his window and listened to the kid talk a mile a minute about how she said it was okay if they all got out of the car to play catch with him. Rhys held her gaze as he slid out of the SUV. He gave her a saucy grin, promising retribution, but they all played along. He and his brothers spread out in the yard and started tossing the ball.

"Can we take this inside?"

"Sure." The woman stepped back inside and moved to stand in front of the window, opening the curtains. "I'm Sadie's mother, Betty."

"What's the boy's name?"

She hesitated.

"Don't worry. I'm not going to tell anyone about his ability." She pulled out her badge and showed it to the woman before re-clipping it to her jeans. "You have my word."

"Gabe."

"Is he Sadie's son?"

"Yes," she answered, never taking her gaze from the yard outside.

"Is she here?"

"She never came home last night, and I haven't been able to reach her today." Only then did the woman turn to face Elizabeth with worry in her eyes. "She's never been this irresponsible. I'm worried."

"When was the last time you talked to her?"

"She called before leaving work. She said was going to the Honey Pot to meet her friends and asked if I could watch

Gabe."

"Who's Gabe's father, and where is he?" Elizabeth asked, picking up a frame on the coffee table that depicted Betty, Sadie, and Gabe.

"Nate Bishop. I don't know how they met, but"—Betty gave a slight shrug— "he took off after changing Sadie into a wolf and knocking her up."

Elizabeth set the picture down. "That doesn't make sense, especially if he got her pregnant. Mates are a protective bunch. That's assuming they were mates."

"Oh, they were mates all right," Betty continued. "No one knows why he left or where he went. He wasn't even decent enough to give her an explanation. He met her, claimed her, knocked her up, and split. He only returned once when Gabe turned four. I caught him in the yard talking to the boy. I threatened to skin him alive if he ever came back."

"I bet Sadie didn't like that."

"She didn't talk to me for a week. She just went to work and came home. If she could have afforded to move out, she would have left and never looked back. But she couldn't afford it with the little salary she's making.

"Where does she work?"

"She works as an aid in the legal department on Senator Hayes' campaign."

"Wait." Lizzie's brows dipped. "Your

daughter is a shifter, correct?"

"Yes."

"Why is she working for a senator who wants to tag the shifter population?"

Betty's face turned guarded, and she pressed her lips together. "I don't know."

Oh yes, she did. She just wasn't saying. Without warning, she did something she wouldn't normally do to an older woman. She blurted out the reason she was there.

"Emily Fisher was found murdered in an alleyway a block from the Honey Pot. She was last seen leaving the club with your daughter. If there is any hope of finding Sadie still alive, I'm going to need you to help. Tell me what you know," Elizabeth pleaded.

Betty turned back to the window, her jaw set in a hardened line. "I can't." She walked to the door and called Gabe back inside. "You have to leave."

Gabe dragged his feet walking back to his grandmother. He stood in front of her, his head hanging down as she rested her arms protectively around his shoulders. "Please, just go."

Elizabeth pulled out two of her business cards and handed one to Betty. "Call me if you can think of anything else."

She squatted in front of Gabe and handed him the other. "You call me if you ever need anything. I know what it's like to be different and scared."

He nodded and took her card.

She stood and gave them a curt nod. She couldn't make the lady tell her anything. As aggravating as it was, she had to walk out the door knowing that there were things the lady wouldn't say. She glanced up at the curtains once more as she climbed into the SUV. Gabe was perched in front of the window. He gave her a wave goodbye.

She waved back even as she spoke. "Sadie was an aid working for the senator. Her mom said that she never came home."

Rhys backed out of the driveway before reaching for her to link their hands. A calming force surrounded her while her mind muddled through what she'd learned so far.

"I told you we could help," Max called out from the back seat.

Glancing over her shoulder, she smiled at the brothers. "Thanks for that. I'm sure Gabe enjoyed it."

She turned back in her seat, her mind returning to the case.

"You're squeezing my hand off. What's bothering you, Lizzie?" Rhys asked. Lifting her fingers to his mouth, he pressed a gentle kiss to her palm.

"Mates," she answered and pulled her hand away.

Chapter 8

"I thought we talked about mating," Rhys answered, giving her a sideways glance.

"Not you and me. Mates in general." She swiveled in her seat so she could see everyone in the SUV. "Why would a wolf leave his mate, especially after he got her pregnant? Isn't that protection gene embedded into you guys when you're born? Isn't that why you start acting like cavemen?"

Rhys glanced in the rearview mirror and hoped one of his brothers might take a stab at answering her question. When they stayed quiet, he spoke up. "It's like this. When our beasts recognize our mates, something just clicks inside of us.

We're protectors; we're lovers; and you, our mates, are our number one priority. Nothing will ever matter more than protecting and loving our mates and making them happy."

"Nice in theory, I guess. But then why would he leave her alone to bring a child into this world?" she asked, genuinely interested in the answer. She spun back in her seat, pressing her lips together, trying to figure out everything in her head. "Assuming your theory is correct."

"It is," he answered and grinned.

She rolled her eyes. "Assuming you are, a mate loves and protects above all else. He loved, and his way of protecting her was to leave. It's the only thing that makes sense. But what the hell was he protecting her from?"

"Maybe himself," Max answered from the backseat.

"Or something he was involved in," Dylan chimed in. "It's possible he didn't want to lead them to her doorstep."

"One thing is for certain," Rhys said and took her hand, entwining their fingers again, not wasting another minute when he could be touching her. "He has to be going out of his mind. In that little space of time when I didn't know where you were, I was ready to tear anyone apart that got in my way. My one and only goal was to find you. I couldn't see beyond that, but that's just me." He glanced at her.

"Let's assume for a second he was worried about leading them to her. I still can't see him walking away for good." Max leaned forward and propped his arms on the back of the seat. "He would have kept tabs, even if he was in danger and couldn't be with her. He would have kept tabs to make sure that she and his son were safe. He would have implemented some type of safeguard. At least, that's what I would have done."

"What kind of safeguard?"

"Someone he trusted to protect her and his kid."

She glanced back. "You think?"

"Oh yeah," Rhys answered.

She turned back around, looking out the window. She looked lost in thought, as if she were contemplating the sins of the world. "Where are we going?"

Rhys held in his grin. "I'm taking Max and Dylan home. They need to get ready for work, and I'm feeding you a late lunch." He glanced her way. "You need to eat."

"Rhys, there are missing women; I can't just stop to eat because you want to play house."

"You're not going to be any good to anyone if you don't take care of yourself, and if you won't do it, then I will."

"You're doing the caveman thing."

"I know. You can call Colton from the house while I make you lunch. We'll make it quick."

Elizabeth pulled out her phone and started typing.

"What are you doing?"

"Sending an email to Colton to put out an APB on the rest of the women."

****

Elizabeth trotted up the stairs to her room and grabbed her laptop out of her backpack before heading back downstairs. She kicked off her shoes and plopped down on to the oversized sofa, settling in as the guys all milled around her. She booted it up and transferred her notes to send to Colton via email. She started a file on each of the girls and typed up what she knew, what she'd been told, and what she'd observed, making sure to put her questions on the page before saving the documents. She still had work to do, no matter what the others were doing. She had no intention of wasting time. Her cell phone rang, and she slid it out of her back pocket and pressed it to her ear. "Hanson."

"Where are you?" Colton growled.

"We just got back to the ranch for a quick bite and to drop off his brothers.

What's up?"

"We had to release Horace. His DNA didn't match."

She heard a door shut in the background before he spoke again. "I've heard rumors that there's been a hit put out on you."

"By Horace?"

"I haven't confirmed who initiated it yet," Colton answered.

"Horace might be hot-headed, but he'd want to do the kill personally." There was no way that mutt would be denied being responsible for her death. She'd humiliated him. Horace coming after her made sense. The hit didn't. She could hold her own against the damn wolf, but that wasn't the question. The question she was left asking herself was, who else wanted her dead? "This hit is from someone else that I've pissed off. We need to figure out who's behind it so I can deal with it. This complicates things."

She tossed the computer next to her and stood, walking out the front door and onto the porch. She eased the door shut behind her. "Before I only had myself to worry about." She glanced at the closed door before stepping off the porch. "Now there are more lives on the line. Maybe I should leave."

All of her caged animals growled below the surface, each begging to be let free so they could tear the threat apart. She ground her teeth together, thinking about anyone hurting Rhys. She'd never let that happen. She clenched the phone tighter in her grip.

"I want you to stay put until we have more information. I'm meeting with one of my informants tonight. So you're benched until tomorrow."

"I can't wait that long. I haven't checked on the other women yet."

"Jennifer Smith has finally been reported as missing." He told her.

"And the others? Have they been reported yet?"

"Yes, but I want you to stay put until the morning. That's an order, Elizabeth. Do you understand?" He asked her, his voice unyielding.

Movement along the tree line caught her eye as the wind blew, so she was slow to answer. "Yep. Loud and clear." She waited longer, scanning the trees to see if she spotted anything or anyone. She inhaled a deep breath. Nothing but the scent of flowers mingled in the wind, their sweet scent coupled with the musky scent of... bear. She clicked the phone off and shoved it into her pocket before turning to find Rhys standing on the porch. His big, strong arms crossed over his chest. His jaw ticked.

"How much of that did you overhear?"

"Leaving, Horace, and that there is a hit out on you," he growled, and his eyes flashed in anger.

She closed the distance between them and placed a reassuring palm on his arm. "I'm not going to get myself killed."

"Damn right, you're not." He cupped her ass and lifted her to his height. Her legs wrapped around his waist and her arms around his neck. Uncontrollable flames ignited in her core, and her panties dampened in need. She'd done a damn fine job at keeping the bear at arms-length, but when he touched her...her mind battled with her body. It was a fight she was slowly losing.

"Put me down. You're acting ridiculous." Her brow rose in challenge.

He carried her back inside, kicking the door shut with his foot before pressing her back against the wood. Her chest rose and fell in anticipation.

His gaze slid over her face and landed on her lips. Need took over. Her beast fought to convince her to take what he offered. She might not be interested in a mate, but she was damn sure interested in a roll in the sack with the man holding her tightly in his arms.

"I'm off the clock for the rest of the night," she whispered and watched in humor as his gaze swirled from blue to a stormy gray.

He pressed his lips to hers, devouring her with heat. Her humor was replaced with desire as a growl of approval rumbled deep in his chest. She parted her lips, opening and offering him what they both wanted, what they both needed. He took control, giving and taking, sipping and deepening, driving every nerve in her body into a frenzy. He pressed into her, and she felt the huge bulge between his legs, leaving no doubt, that if given the green light, he would take her pressed up against the door, not caring that his brothers might see. She'd never wanted another man more than she wanted Rhys in this very minute. She broke the kiss and nuzzled his neck, leaving both her animals and his bear purring to life. She wasn't ready for a mate, but damn, she wanted to feel him, have him, and hold him. Like nothing she'd ever wanted before.

Her stomach let out an awkward growl. Heat seared her cheeks, not from her hunger, but because she'd let herself get carried away.

"You need food."

"Yes, food," she repeated, thankful that her stomach broke the chemistry. She unlocked her legs and slowly slid down his rock-hard body. His hands stayed on her waist until her feet touched the floor.

"I'll cook, and you can tell me all about

how there's a contract out on your life." He slid his fingers through hers and led the way into the empty kitchen. He released her only to pull marinating steaks out of the fridge, along with two beers. He popped the top and handed her one before walking out onto the back deck to ignite the grill. She followed and hopped up on the wood railing, watching him work.

"How about we talk about something else?"

He glanced at her and lit the coals, waiting for the little black squares to turn white. "We're still having the conversation about the hit, but I'll bite for now. What do you want to talk about?"

"Who's the oldest out of you and your brothers?"

"I am. Max is the baby, and Dylan is the middle cub."

"Are your parents still alive?"

"No," he answered, gingerly poking at the coals. "I was fifteen when they were slaughtered by hunters. Colton's mother took us in. That's why we're so close to our cousin."

"I'm sorry."

"It was a long time ago." He shrugged walking back into the house and grabbing the steaks. He dropped them onto the grill and shut the lid, leaning his hip on the rail next to her. One hand held her leg as if worried she might fall backward and the other was holding the beer to his lips as he drank. All of his little touches meant to reassure her did more than that. They set her body straight into overdrive.

"Remove your hand, or we won't be eating." She bit her bottom lip at the same time her stomach growled.

His brows dipped. No doubt the sound of her hungry belly was the only reason he removed his hand. Feeding her seemed more important than seeking out her heat. "Anything else you want to know?"

"Do you want kids?"

His lips twisted at the corners. "I'd like a couple of cubs running around, but I guess that depends on you."

"You were good with Gabe." She gave a small smile and conceded by touching his arm.

"Do you want children?"

She hopped down from the railing and took a long swig of her beer, moving to sit in one of the lounge chairs. "Once upon a time, I did. Now, not so much."

"What changed your mind?" He raised the lid on the grill and turned the steaks.

She chewed her bottom lip, not sure what to tell him. If he knew the truth, would he still want her? Still desire her if he knew the crud coursing in her veins? "I..."

The crack of a branch had her scanning the tree line and sniffing the air.

Slowly, she rose from her seat and gripped the railing. The hair on her neck stood up to take notice, and her animals started to pace. She blinked, and her vision turned red while scanning the surrounding scenery, looking for what her human eyes couldn't see. Nothing but large trees and thick brush covered the grounds. It was quiet. The crickets no longer chirped, and the birds took flight at once, soaring out of the trees and high into the sky.

"What's back there?"

"About fifty acres of forest, a stream, and a pond," he answered, and they both sniffed at the same time. This time she caught their faint scent. Her lips lifted in a predatory grin.

"Wolves," they said at the same time.

"Go inside and lock the door," Rhys growled, pulling the shirt off of his body, ready to shift.

"As if. This is my fight."

She ripped the holster off her leg and shifted on the spot, not knowing or caring which of her animals emerged, as long as it was one big, bad-ass animal that could fight off a wolf attack. Long teeth slid out of her gums. The clothes ripped at the seams and dropped from her body as her bones extended and cracked before shrinking and contorting, snapping into place. The magic of the shift surrounded her, consuming her into her core, leaving her momentarily breathless. She dropped to all fours and shook her body, twitching her whiskers. She glanced down at her paws. Orange and brown stripes instead of orange and black. She wasn't just a tiger. She was a Siberian. She'd wanted a bad-ass animal, and she got one. She opened her mouth, and a loud, angry roar rolled from deep in her gut.

Her bear growled, and she padded alongside of him, rubbing her face along his leg. They were both predators, and if they'd been in any other situation, she might dare call them enemies, but not tonight, not him, never him.

She ran in front of him, stopping just inside the tree line. Adjusting her vision, she scanned the woods while she paced. Her claws dug into the dirt, waiting, watching for the first wolf to appear. She sniffed the air and crouched low, ready to attack.

Five wolves stepped out from the trees, surrounding them, but none of them were Horace. She'd know his stink anywhere, and yet he wasn't among this group of soon-to-be-dead wolves.

Bring it on, bitches. She purred in delight at the anticipation of blood on her lips.

Her bear stepped in front of her, blocking her from the wolves, and she nipped at his heels. Two wolves leaped toward him at once, one from the right and the other from the left. He caught one in a bear hug and squeezed as the wolf went for his neck. She caught the other wolf in mid jump, knocking him out of the air and landing on him with her 350-pound body. She sank her teeth into his neck and easily ripped into him, tearing the tendons and flesh. Blood coated her tongue and teeth, the coppery liquid sending her beast into a frenzy. It wanted to kill, to destroy. She licked her lips and eyed the remainder of the wolves, waiting to see who would be next.

Her bear had two more on him. One he batted down with his large, clawed paws, leaving gashes down the wolf's belly. He howled in pain. The other wolf was clinging to Rhys' back, his claws sunk deep into his pelt. Without a second thought, she jumped and ripped the wolf off, flinging him to the ground with her teeth embedded into his neck. He clawed and yapped and growled, getting one good slash at her shoulder before she tore out his throat. He gurgled around the gushing blood. Four down and more were appearing from the woods, surrounding them. One would fall, and two more would take his place.

Licking the blood from her whiskers, she scanned the trees looking for her next victim, the last big fucker with black hair that had dared to attack them first. He was nowhere to be found. She sniffed the air, catching the doggie stench on her whiskers a second too late.

He landed on her back with a thump. His teeth dug into her neck. Her bear's roar vibrated through the ground. The acrid smell of her own blood drifted to her nose. She wasn't about to die, not from this asshole. His teeth tore at her flesh, not loosening his hold, so she did the one thing she could think of, not having ever been in this skin before. She was a heavy bitch, and it was time she used her size to her advantage. She dropped to her belly and rolled with the bastard on her back, squishing him under her. The sound of bones cracking beneath her made her kitty purr, and the wolf's bite slacken. It took her a second to get to her paws. She snarled, ready to finish the kill at the same time the man from the video, the one who had followed the girls from the club, Evan, jumped down from the tree with a sword in his hand.

"Help the bear," he ordered. Lifting the blade in the air, he plunged it directly into the wolf's heart.

She leapt on the nearest wolf, clawing and ripping her way through the crowd toward Rhys. Her cramping, sore muscles screamed in protest, but she wouldn't stop—she'd never stop—not until she reached him.

He was destroying the wolves, making a path directly toward her until they were side by side. The remaining wolves left standing were pacing like caged animals. The leader of this attack lay dead at their feet.

Who's next?

She rubbed against Rhys' leg, reassuring him she was fine. Crimson blood matted his black fur as she paced at his feet in a protective shield, daring any others to get too close.

Evan stepped closer to her, and her bear roared and lifted his long claws, ready to strike. She stood between Rhys and Evan and the wolves debating which enemy was more of a threat. She inched against Rhys' legs, easing him backward and farther away. The wolves let out a long howl before charging off into the woods, being chased away by two bears lumbering into the woods, standing on two legs as they spotted her tiger and prepared to fight.

They roared a menacing growl at her tiger, and Rhys let out an even louder, deadly growl back in challenge. He turned his back to her, to protect her from his brothers, as she kept her back to him, to protect him from Evan.

Evan sheathed his sword in the holder on his back before dropping to his knees and bowing his head. "Shift, Abigail. I will not harm you. The other bears need to see who you are."

Elizabeth shifted, standing nude in the clearing, not caring that Evan was a stranger. She reached behind her, holding onto Rhys' pelt in reassurance. Her body trembled, and her breathing was harsh. She clung to him.

He changed instantly and pushed her behind him so that he was the one facing Evan. His brothers, finally realizing who she was and that she was no longer a threat, started to shift.

"Elizabeth, baby, you're shaking. Go put on my shirt. Evan isn't going anywhere." Rhys growled not taking his gaze from Evan.

"Don't kill him," she rested her palm on his arm. "He helped us."

"You will come to no harm from me, Abigail," Evan acknowledged.

Rhys glanced back at her and raised his brow before blocking Evan from view. "Abigail?"

She didn't answer, just peered around Rhys, narrowing her gaze. Elizabeth jogged back to the deck, grabbed her weapon and pulled on Rhys' shirt, which hung down to her knees. She raised the shirt to her nose and inhaled. His sweet, honey musk infused her, surrounding her with everything Rhys. She returned to the clearing within minutes. They were all still standing, staring at each other, tension thick in the darkening sky.

She raised her gun and aimed it at Evan's chest. "How do you know my name?"

He tilted his head. "I wasn't aware you'd learned to use firearms, Abigail."

"Answer the damn question." She cocked the hammer.

"Who the hell is Abigail?" Rhys demanded.

"I was," she answered keeping her focus on Evan.

Chapter 9

"You still are. You'll never outrun your destiny." Evan took a step in her direction, and Elizabeth aimed the gun a foot in front of his boots and pulled the trigger.

The shit head didn't even jump.

"That was the only warning you'll get, asshole. Not another step or the next one is through the heart."

"I'm your guard," he answered. "My job is to protect and guide you."

"I'm her protector," Rhys growled and stepped up beside her.

Evan made a gesture to the blood soaking Rhys' shirt from the wound at her shoulder. "She's bleeding. You both are.

We need to take this in the house so I can tend to her."

"If you'd like to keep your hands, I'd suggest letting Rhys tend to her," Max advised, stepping forward with Dylan flanking him.

There was way too much testosterone aimed at her in the clearing. Not to mention that she was seeing more of Rhys' brothers than should be legally allowed.

Rhys tenderly brushed the shirt to the side to see the damage left by the bite marks at her shoulder. They were already healing because of her shift. She touched the wound, her fingertips coming away sticky and wet, yet she felt no pain from the wound thanks to the adrenaline pumping through her body.

"Let's get you cleaned up." He swept her off her feet. She squealed in protest, bound in his embrace, while he carried her back toward the house. "Bring him inside," he called over his shoulder.

"Put me down. I can walk."

"I know," he answered, holding her tighter, careful of her shoulder. He pressed a lingering kiss to her head. "I'll put you down when we're inside, Abigail."

"Call me that one more time and it's you who will need patching up, bear." Elizabeth rolled her eyes but settled into his embrace. "My name is Elizabeth. Abigail died years ago."

Rhys carried her straight into the house, ignoring the burning steaks still on the grill.

She glanced over his shoulder longingly at the black smoke rising from the grill. "The assholes ruined our food." She pouted.

He grinned. "Don't worry. I'll feed my kitty some meat." He took the stairs two at a time, which was impressive with her in his arms. "You could have told me your animal was a tiger."

"Well...." She snapped her lips closed. The Siberian tiger may have been one of her animals, but she had a crap load more that could have just as easily made an appearance. "There's a lot more I need to tell you."

He stomped through the room directly into the bathroom, putting her down on the counter between the double sinks.

"You don't need to go to all this trouble. I'm sure it's healed by now." Without thinking twice, she pulled the shirt off and set it beside her, twisting her torso to get a better look at the scratch in the mirror. It was on the same side as the mark Boris left on her.

"I know you're new to shifting into an animal, but we don't just heal completely because we shift."

"I do," she answered matter-of-factly, not sure what to make of the fact that others didn't. Was that just another anomaly that separated her from the others?

Rhys used a wet washcloth to wipe away the blood. He paused, resting his hands on her legs, looking at her freshly knit skin. His mouth parted and he just stared at her shoulder. The same side of her body where the scars Boris had given her had knit back together, leaving only a light pink scar where the tear had once been. "I don't..."

He lightly touched the year-old scar on her shoulder, and heat flushed her skin. She was sitting entirely naked in front of her mate for the first time. A single touch and flames licked her veins, making her throb at her core. Her nipples pebbled, begging for his touch.

"Who did this to you?" he asked. His lips dipped into a frown.

"A dead bear," she answered placing her hand over his. She slowly moved his fingers in a path over her collarbone until they rested on her breast. Whether it was the adrenaline from the fight or just the fact that her mate was standing between her legs and naked as the day he was born, she didn't care. She traced the muscles on his chest and arms, exploring him for the first time, pulling her deeper into a lust-filled haze.

She reached between his legs and

stroked her thumb over the head of his shaft. Running her fingers down his length, she gripped him and pulled in long, even strokes.

"Elizabeth." Her name came out as a growl deep in his chest as he lowered his head, running his wet tongue around her rosy nipple. He scraped his teeth along the tender flesh before sucking it deep into his mouth. His hand stilled hers on his shaft, and he pulled it away to rest at his side before cupping her other breast, running his thumb over the peak.

Fuck....the sensations consumed her, reminding her of all of the feelings she'd given up.

"Oh god." She moaned, scraping her nails in a light path down his back. She needed to be closer. She needed to feel him.

One last lick and he raised his head, locking his gaze with hers. He pulled her closer to the counter's edge. Hunger, desire, and everything she'd never known she wanted looked back at her. He leaned in and kissed her in the hollow of her throat, leaving a tender swipe with his tongue before raising his head again. His normally blue eyes were stormy and dark gray. His cock pressed at her heat, rubbing through her juices. He stood unmoving.

"Tell me you want this."

She wrapped her legs around his waist and used her heels to inch him closer.

"More than anything." She hardly recognized her own husky voice. "I need you, Rhys."

He reached between them and used the pad of his thumb, circling on her clit. He pressed a finger into her juices, and she clenched it tight. Her head fell back on her shoulders, and she moaned, clutching his shoulders tightly. She was close, so damn close.

He eased his finger in and out and added two more, stretching her as his mouth latched onto her other breast, suckling and scraping his teeth against her sensitive flesh. His fingers quickened, and every muscle in her body clenched, trying to fight off the rising orgasm about to consume her.

"Oh yes, faster." She moaned. "More."

He twisted his fingers and pressed deliciously against her G-spot while his thumb pressed on her clit. Colors exploded behind her closed eyes. She said his name, her voice coming out raspy from heat. Her body shivered in convulsions as her channel tightened on his fingers. He continued to stroke her, easing her down from the ledge.

She rested her head on his shoulder and kissed his neck. Every muscle in her body relaxed into his hold. Pulling his fingers free, he licked her juices from his fingers, moaning at her taste.

"Your turn," she whispered and guided his shaft to her sex.

He pressed in, seating himself in one full stroke. She moaned and clenched his arms, scratching his arms with her nails. She raised her hips, needing him to move, needing all of him, more of him.

He eased in and out, leaning over her, deliciously pressing her clit with each stroke. Her orgasm built again, and his extra-large cock grew thicker inside of her, touching and stretching, claiming and demanding her to accommodate him.

A growl formed deep in his chest. "Damn, baby. I'm not going to last this first time." He pressed into her harder, lifting her legs over his arms and holding her open for his view. He pumped in and out of her, making her take everything he had to give. "Fuck, you're such a pretty pussy cat." He reached between them and circled her bud once again. "You're coming with me, baby." He grunted out each word as her orgasm built, growing, tightening against his throbbing cock.

"Oh yes, Rhys."

"That's my girl. Feel me, baby. This is yours, all yours."

The combination of his words, his finger and his strokes sent her over the top. He dropped her legs and leaned over her. His lips pressed to hers in a searing crush, and he swallowed the scream of his name, not slowing until she felt his release. His hot seed shot, filling her channel until they both collapsed in a whimpering, sweaty mass of bodies pressed intimately together.

His rapid heartbeat slowed, matching hers. He lowered his head, pressing a lingering, sweet kiss to her lips. "I'm sleeping with you tonight."

She chuckled. "What about waiting for an invite?"

He eased an inch out of her before pushing in again. She felt him growing by the second.

"Am I not invited?"

He stroked her again.

"Oh yeah, you're invited."

He pressed another kiss to her neck before pulling free.

"We need to get cleaned up so we can go deal with Evan."

She closed her eyes and leaned her head back against the mirror. "You're right."

Fifteen minutes later, after a quick shower, she felt better than she had all day. Her muscles were boneless and sated until she followed Rhys back down the stairs, and she instantly felt the aggravation coming from Evan.

"Enjoy yourself, Abigail?" he asked

with a raised brow.

She glanced at him and narrowed her eyes, stepping down the last five steps. "Call me that again. I dare you."

He held her gaze, unrepentant, yet to his credit, he was smart enough not to say her name again. "What happened to the girls from the club?" she asked, standing at the bottom of the stairs.

He didn't reply, just kept a watchful gaze on the occupants of the room.

"Fine, let's start with an easier question. How do you know the name Abigail?"

"Because I've known about you since the day you were born."

She rested a fist on her waist. Her whole body was strung tight. She was ready to explode at the first, wrong word. "Yeah?" she spat out. "As my protector, right? Isn't that what you said?"

She gritted her teeth and lifted her chin. The more she thought about what he was saying, the more pissed off she became.

"Always." He bowed his head.

"Then where the hell were you a year ago?" She lunged for Evan, ready to strangle the lies from his throat.

"There is much you don't know."

Rhys caught her in his warm, strong embrace. He wrapped her into his arms, pulling her back against his chest as if sensing she needed the restraint.

He placed a tender, calming kiss on her neck, and her anger returned to a simmer, waiting for the temperature to kick in. "He's lying."

"Unhand her, bear," Evan demanded in a deadly tone, rising to stand in front of the fireplace. "My job is to protect you, Abigail, even if it's from yourself. He is not your mate."

She chuckled at his words. Maybe it was her nerves, her agitation, maybe even the sex she'd just had, or hell, it could have been from the deathly stare Evan was giving her, but she couldn't help herself. She let the giggle building inside spill from her lips. Anger and agitation about this whole new feeling ripped through her. Here was this maniac telling her not to trust the only man, besides Trapp, who'd ever helped her, who'd ever vowed to make her happy. Who she was learning to...like. She hadn't wanted a mate, but now...Being told that Rhys wasn't hers? That just aggravated the piss out of her. What the hell did this schmuck think she was going to do? Trust him? Her whole body shook as she laughed at the situation. The attack, Evan, hell, even Horace coming after her. She continued to laugh hysterically until tears slipped free from her eyes.

They all watched her as though she'd

grown a second head, but their confused looks just made her laugh even harder until she snorted, and that sound had her doubling over at the waist laughing even more.

"Did you tell him?" Evan asked, stepping closer.

She righted, swiping at her tears, taking deep, long breaths to push away the humor that only she apparently felt from the situation.

Dylan and Max moved across the room closer to her and Rhys, as if waiting for Evan to attack.

"Tell him what? That you're missing a few screws? I think that's pretty obvious." She cleared her throat, trying not to smile.

He clicked his tongue and folded his arms over his black sleeveless leather vest. The top of his muscled arms were covered in some type of intricate tribal tattoos. Others might call her stupid for baiting this man, but she was past the point of caring what anyone thought. Evan was surrounded by a roomful of bears...and her.

"That the cat isn't your only animal, that they're all part of you." He growled. "I saved you when you were taken."

Elizabeth's mouth parted at his words, and heat flooded her cheeks. She moved out of Rhys' embrace, calling on the strength of her dragon that would tear apart Evan's lies. She stepped toward the intruder, the man no longer welcome in this house. "Saved me? I don't remember anyone putting a stop to those needles being shoved in my arms." She took another step closer, grinding her teeth, the muscles in her shoulders strung tight. "Or when Boris was trying to tear out my throat...or hell, when I was on the verge of dying from all of that foreign DNA mixing in my veins. No...I don't recall seeing you anywhere nearby, you delusional prick."

"How easily we forget." He answered.

She was standing directly in front of Evan, daring him to make a move, daring him to shift into anything so she'd be justified for killing the asshole just like she'd done to the scientist that had tried to kill her soul.

"Elizabeth."

Rhys' warm palms rested on her waist. He'd moved in behind her, and she felt his warmth radiating and surrounding her like a blanket on a cold winter's day, calming her anger once again, in a way only he could. He eased her body back into his chest. His move was such a natural thing and yet unfamiliar to her.

Evan's jaw ticked. His eyes flicked from mossy green to deep black like the pits of hell before returning to green. "You might not have seen me, but I *was* there. I switched the vials they filled you with. If it hadn't been for me, you would have died. They would have stripped away and killed every animal you have, leaving you nothing but a shell. That was their plan all along. You and you alone were the target. The other women that were taken were merely test subjects. It was you who they planned to make into a killing machine, and if that didn't work, they'd planned to destroy you. Did you honestly think that it was possible for a normal human to survive all of that DNA?"

She remained silent. Her eyes flashed, changing the color of the room red in her vision.

"They pumped you full of your own blood, Abigail. That wasn't a coincidence. It's your own blood coursing through your veins."

"This doesn't make any sense. Why me? And how was it my own blood?"

A shimmer of something flashed in his eyes before he quickly masked it. "Because of who you are. You don't you remember?" His words softened. "I promised to help you escape."

Recognition of his voice made her pause. "You didn't stop the bear? Because of you, I almost died."

"The bear that used his bite to infect you with his enzymes was a stupid fuck. It was never his bite you had to worry about killing you. He'd ingested the enzymes in your blood and would have died within a month had you not already taken care of it yourself." He stepped closer to her. "No, sweetheart, if I hadn't intervened, you would most definitely be dead from the crap they had planned for you. There was a reason why I had access to your blood. They took it from you, and they studied it."

"You were one of them?" Elizabeth felt the muscles in Rhys' arm growing tense with the more this asshole shared. Soon her secrets would be all out in the open.

"The games they played did nothing more than bring out your true identity; so in reality, they did you a favor by awakening you from the damn sleep you were in...It didn't kill Abigail. It brought her to life for the first time ever."

"That's not possible." Elizabeth's words were a breath between them. Confusion clouded her brain. Rhys took a step back, taking her with him.

"You were supposed to be told." Evan ran his hand through his hair. "On your twenty-fifth birthday, your uncle was supposed to prepare you for what to expect when you returned to us. Shit."

"What the hell are you talking about; I don't have an uncle." She screamed.

Dylan interrupted her argument. "I called Trapp. He's on his way."

"Abigail..."

"That is not my name!" she yelled. Something inside her snapped, and she swung, her fist making contact with Evan's nose. She heard the crunch of his bones as his face whipped to the side. He slowly turned to face her; his glowing red eyes matched the blood from his busted lip.

"Want to play hardball?" He narrowed his eyes. "Fine. I thought it would help to ease you into this information, but no." He rubbed his jaw and narrowed his eyes. "You, princess, are a natural-born descendant of the royal line of Jordanians. They're a sacred breed of ancient shifters whose main mission in life is protection. You don't have *one* animal to call your own. They are *all* yours, and I *am* your guard."

"Nice job you're doing." Her lips curled. She turned her back on the crazy man. She cupped Rhys' face and pressed a kiss to his lips. "You can deal with him. I'm starved." She winked before she sidestepped him, heading for the kitchen. She paused at the threshold and glanced over her shoulder. "You were wrong about one thing, Guardian." The word dripped with hatred and distrust. "Rhys *is* my mate and is more of a protector than you'll ever be."

"Your father has called you home."

She clenched the door frame at his

words. Ice skirted down her spine and through her veins.

She slowly turned in place to face the liar. "My father is dead."

"The human man who raised you is dead. He was your uncle, killed by the same people that abducted you. He's the one that failed to explain things to you before you turned twenty-five. It's not his royal blood coursing through your veins that gave you life."

She ground her teeth. If Trapp didn't get here soon, he'd be staring at a dead suspect in the women's abductions. "I have his eyes," she countered, her words a whisper in the quiet room. "And my mother's temper." Her voice was becoming louder. "There is no way that you will ever convince me that the man who raised me was not my father, so you can save your breath." Her nostrils flared, her vision flashed red, and her nails lengthened without a shift.

"Your father was a twin. One was to be king, the other a commoner among mortal men."

Rhys growled at the accusation, but her anger eased.

This man was mental. He was sick. That was the only explanation she could form. "Assuming this breed even exists, you're trying to tell me that the Jordanian King let a commoner raise one of his children?"

"His only child." He bowed and lifted his arm across his chest in a weird salute. "Princess Abigail. Your father sent you to live with his brother so you could understand exactly what you were meant to fight for. You weren't supposed to find out until you were ready. You alone can save both of our kinds."

"Great," she mumbled. "Well, I hate to break it to you, but I can't even locate three women that went missing from a nightclub, much less know how to save not one but two races. Well, go ahead and kiss your ass goodbye. We're all doomed." She glanced toward her mate, the one she still hadn't legally claimed. "Rhys, I'm going to fix a sandwich and check the woods for any lingering animals. Will you tell me when Trapp arrives?"

"Max, Dylan." He gave them a nod to follow her.

"I'll call Marcus to open the bar." Dylan's brows dipped.

"I'll make the food." Max started pulling things out of the fridge.

Chapter 10

Elizabeth took a bite of her sandwich as Max and Dylan followed her into the woods. Evan escaping from a mental institution was the only answer she could come up with. The only thing left of the shifters' dead bodies was little more than white ash scattered in the dirt and on the green fallen leaves. When a shifter died, the myth was true that it turned back into its human shell; what wasn't known was why some continued disintegrating until nothing was left but ash.

Evan couldn't be telling the truth. It just didn't make sense. None of it did. She wasn't a royal. She didn't have or need a protector now, and even if there was a speck of truth to Evan's claims, there was no way in hell she'd return to a father who had thrown her out like the trash. Nope. She shook her head. Colton Trapp could deal with this dipwad. She had more pressing things to worry about, like who was abducting the women and where the heck they were being held.

That thought had her pausing mid-step. She spun around to face the house. "Evan knew."

"Knew what, Lizzie?" Max asked.

"He knew my past. He knew about the lab, the vials..." She let her thoughts trail off.

"Even if he knew some of whatever happened to you, why act as your protector now? Why not before when it sounded like it mattered most?" Dylan shrugged and kicked around the leaves, looking for clues as to who might have sent the shifters.

"I'm not talking about my past. He followed the missing girls out of the club." Her mouth parted. He had the answers she needed to break this damn case.

Elizabeth left the boys in their search and jogged up to the house. Flinging the back door open, she stomped inside.

Evan was pinned against the wall with Rhys' fingers wrapped around his throat. "Put me down, bear, before I have to kill you, and then she'll really get pissed at me."

"I'd like to see you try." Rhys banged Evan even harder against the wall.

"What the hell are you two doing?" Elizabeth demanded through gritted teeth. "Rhys, drop him. And Evan... don't you dare threaten him again, or I don't care who the hell you are, I'll kill you myself."

"You don't need to fight my battles, Lizzie," Rhys growled and released his hold. Evan dropped into a crouch. His muscles strung tight.

"She's the only reason you're still breathing, bear," Evan choked out as he stood.

"What happened?" she demanded.

Evan prodded. "You might as well tell her."

"Your Guard claims that he's destined to be your mate," Rhys growled.

Elizabeth's gaze shot to Evan's as she moved to stand beside Rhys. She entwined their fingers in a reassuring grip. "Now I know you're on crack. I can feel the pull between Rhys and me. Hell, I can't even deny that. You can't even explain it, other than what happens between mates."

Rhys glanced down at her, letting go of her hand. He cupped her face and held her gaze. Lowering his head, he pressed a kiss to her lips. He understood what she'd just said. Her words weren't to appease anyone other than herself. She'd meant what she said, regardless if they'd yet to seal the deal. Rhys cared about her. He might not love her yet, but there was potential where once there had been nothing but a dismal, empty shell of a life for her. He brought color and feelings into her life when everything she'd felt had been stolen from her a year ago. Spending one day with Rhys might not have convinced her she loved him, but she knew she cared and that he cared about her, which was more than Evan could argue.

Evan's lips twisted at the corners. "You haven't claimed him, and he hasn't claimed you."

"How do you know that?"

"It's a full moon tonight. If he'd bitten you or you him, then he'd be dead. It's part of your genetics," Evan answered, not in a threat but as if it was a natural response.

"I've known him less than forty-eight hours," She whispered as she turned back to Evan.

She heard the car pull up without even having to look out the window. "Rhys, I need a few minutes alone with Evan."

"Are you sure?" Worry clouded his gaze.

She cupped his face. "I'm sure. Colton is about to drag him down to the precinct, and I need a few minutes to ask him my own questions."

He ran the pad of his thumb across her lips before walking out the front door to buy her some time.

She had to work quickly. She spun around to face Evan. "You followed the women out of the club. You knew about me and the lab. My guess is you know exactly who is behind the abductions and where they're holding these women."

Evan raised his brow but didn't answer her question. "Finally piece it together, did you?"

"Why are they doing this?"

"To destroy you and all of our kind."

"Where is it?" she demanded.

He shook his head. "I told you earlier. I am your protector, even if that means protecting you from yourself. You go to that lab, and you'll die." He said it as if he'd seen the future.

"If I don't go to that lab, the other missing women will," she countered.

"Those women are not my concern. You are."

"Listen here." She stepped toward him and ground her teeth together. "I'm going to find that lab, with or without you, and destroy it," she said through clenched teeth. "Then I'm going to find the people responsible and destroy them." She narrowed her eyes. "That is *my* concern."

He lifted his hand to rest on her cheek. She shivered at his touch. "I recognize that fight and fire in your eyes."

She grabbed his hand, squeezing with all of her might as she twisted it behind his back and shoved him into the wall. "Then you know what I said is true," she said, leaning into his back, she pulled his arm unnaturally higher up his back pegging him in place. "Don't touch me again."

"You'll be begging for my touch, princess." He glanced back at her with a cocky smile, so she twisted his arm higher and watched as sweat beaded on his brow.

"You may say that you're saving me from myself, but who is going to save you from me, asshole?"

The door flew open, and Colton stood in the doorway. "Abigail, let the Jordanian go before you get hurt."

Elizabeth swung her gaze to her boss as Evan chuckled. Her mouth parted. "He's lying. He isn't my guard."

Colton clasped his hands together. "Yes, he is."

"Sir?" She released Evan with a little shove and stepped back. A lump formed in her throat.

"How do you think they found you in that alley? I led them to you and explained your importance. You had lost too much blood, and I had to give you some of mine." Evan answered the question she'd yet to ask as he stretched and straightened his arm.

Her heart felt as though it was caving in. Colton Trapp, the one man that she trusted more than anyone, stood in front of her not denying Evan's accusation. Elizabeth took an unconscious step back. This couldn't be happening. Her whole life, her job...a lie. She covered her mouth with her hand as tears swelled in her eyes. "I trusted you."

"I haven't lied to you."

"That's true." Evan shrugged. "An omission of the truth isn't a lie. Not really."

"Shut up," she yelled at Evan. It was his fault her world was crumbling, his fault her secret had surfaced.

"Elizabeth," Rhys called to her and stepped in her direction.

"No," she said angrily, holding up her hand. "Not another step." She shook her head as her heart shattered into a million pieces. Was it possible Rhys knew? Hell, was it possible that Colton had sent her on this mission knowing that Rhys could be her mate? Acid churned in her belly and bile rose to her throat.

She needed to get out of here. She had to go, somewhere, anywhere that she could think. She lifted her chin and straightened her shoulders, grabbing her laptop from the table. She headed for the stairs to grab her keys and her bags. "I'm done here."

"Hanson," Colton's demand made her stop on the third stair. "You aren't leaving. That's a direct order."

She glanced over her shoulder. "Just try and stop me."

She took the stairs two at a time and grabbed her things, including her keys, not giving Rhys enough time to block her exit.

She stomped back down the stairs to find Evan sitting on the couch, his ankle resting on his knee in a casual posture. His muscular arm was stretched out on the back of the couch cushions. A smug-ass smile was on his face, and in any other circumstances, she would have wiped the floor with him because of a smile like that. Now, she just wanted to leave.

Rhys stepped in front of her. "Don't do this. Don't go."

She swallowed around the lump in her throat. "If what you said in the car about my happiness is true, then you won't ask me to stay."

He dropped his head but not his hold on her arm. "Lizzie."

"I'm sorry, Rhys," she said, stepping around him and heading for the door where Colton was still standing. "I just can't...not right now."

"Elizabeth," he growled.

"I'm going to find these women. I'm going to nail the bastards to the wall, and when I'm done, I don't ever want to see you again, Trapp. Consider this my two weeks' notice. I'm done with you and your secrets." She glanced over at Evan, the man who called himself a protector. "And you can go to hell. Consider yourself fired from being my protector, if you ever were."

Elizabeth pulled the door open and walked out of the house, leaving all three men behind her. She'd meant everything she said. She got in her car and headed toward the main road, not stopping until she was a mile away. Tears clouded her vision as she gripped the steering wheel in a punishing hold.

"I'm so stupid," she whispered as she closed her eyes. Visions of Rhys' hurt face stared back at her. And for the first time since she'd escaped the lab, she rested her head on her steering wheel and let the tears consume her. Her body shook as tears streamed down her face. Her heart cracked open into a million pieces. She had nowhere to go, no one she trusted. Not only was there a hit on her life, but she also still had a job to do. The other women's lives depended on it.

Elizabeth sat up and swiped the tears from her eyes. She pulled back out onto the road and did the one thing she was good at. She disappeared under the darkness of night to find a hotel and come up with a plan of action that included trusting no one but herself.

Chapter 11

Rhys shoved Colton against the door, pinning him by his chest. His stomach churned with anxiety and frustration. His bear clawed for purchase to break free like a volcano ready to erupt, taking out everyone in his path. "What the hell did you do?"

A shadow of annoyance crossed Colton's face. His clenched mouth tightened. His arrogant, demanding demeanor was cracking at the edges.

Evan watched in mild amusement from his spot on the couch. "He withheld information from her."

"How could you? She fucking trusted you. Do you realize what you've done?"

Colton shoved Rhys away and stretched his neck from side to side. "I know exactly what I've done." Colton walked past him and moved to stand in front of the fireplace. "I've pissed her off."

"Is it true?" Max asked from the archway in the kitchen. His arms were crossed over his chest. "Did you know about her past all along? About her heritage and her Guard?" He gritted out the last word.

His brother's anger was a welcome reprieve. Finally, someone understood the severity of what had just happened. She'd run because of Colton's deception. There was no way in hell she'd trust Rhys now.

"Yes," Colton answered. "But she's more than a princess, more than my best detective."

"Damn right she is; she's *my* damn mate," Rhys growled, daring any of them to contradict his words. His bear would tear them apart, starting with Evan and his unchecked glare.

"You don't understand," Colton said and started pacing the living room. "When I found her...." He glanced at Evan. "When he showed me where to find her...she was...dying."

Colton ran a hand through his hair and turned to Rhys. "She shifted into a phoenix, shimmering back into human at the last second."

"That's impossible," Rhys said, rubbing at the knots in his neck. "The story of the phoenix is just a myth, and even if it isn't, it's believed they're reborn after death. She would be a child now if that were the case."

"That's where I come in," Evan announced and stood up from where he'd been lounging on the couch. "Abigail..."

"Elizabeth," Rhys growled.

"Elizabeth," Evan conceded. "Due to her abilities, it takes more than a mortal man to protect her. She was already practically immortal due to her mother's phoenix blood, but when she shifted back into her human form, I knew she was giving up. Even as ingrained as her soul was to switch to whatever animal could best save her, she'd unconsciously chosen to go back into her human body and was prepared to die. As her protector, I had to do something to save her. She was more than just my charge or assignment. When I told you we were connected, it's because we are. I gave her my blood and willed her to live."

Rhys growled from across the room. "You turned her? Into what? Just what in the hell are you?"

"That's hard to explain. I'm an immortal tied to Elizabeth's soul."

A tense silence enveloped the room as Evan answered and merely tilted his head.

"In her shifter state, if Ab— Elizabeth dies, she takes with her more than just herself. She takes me."

"If you're immortal, how is that even possible? No matter what happens to her, you would just continue living."

"It's like someone hits a reset button and my life starts over so I grow up with her and her experiences so I can sympathize with the same issues she's dealing with. When she was dying, and I gave her my blood, I willed her to live, and that changed her into more than the shifter she was. She's now an immortal like I am. We're merely like you would imagine vampires to be. We still live, eat and breathe, and we can be killed, it's just harder to do. We're connected by more than blood and life; we're also connected by soul."

"That's impossible," Rhys whispered.

"I can feel her, even when she's not around. When she left, she was devastated. Crying until anger and determination replaced the feeling of despair." Evan folded his arms over his chest. "Let me be clear. Nothing and no one will stop her from finding those women, and until I train her how to protect herself, she will die trying."

"If instinctively she knows to change into animals, how was it possible they caught her and kept her before?" Rhys asked.

"Her abilities were dormant. She didn't even know she had them. I was already working to bring the organization down from the inside when they brought her in. She didn't realize she could shift until after she escaped."

Rhys ran his hand over his face and let out a deep breath, trying to suppress the shimmer beneath his skin and keep his bear under control. "I need to find her."

Colton placed his hand on his back. "Rhys. I'm sorry. She needs to rest tonight. You can find her tomorrow. We already know where she'll be. She emailed me her notes. She still has to interview Jennifer Smith's family."

"I know where she is," Evan announced. He closed green eyes, and when he opened them, they weren't green or black like before but a bright white, void of pupils. He held up his hands. "She just turned into the Valley Fox Hotel." He blinked again, and his eyes returned to their original color.

"How does that trick work?" Max asked, stepping farther into the room.

"We're connected. She to me, and me to her. When I concentrate, I can sense where she is, and most of the times, see what she's seeing."

"Why most? Why not all?" Colton asked.

"She doesn't realize when she's doing it, but it's possible for her to block me."

"That's the best damn thing I've heard you say since you showed up." Rhys knocked away Colton's hand and grabbed his keys from the table without bothering to say anything as he left. Elizabeth might not think she needed him, but damn it, he needed her.

****

Rhys called in a dinner order to the local diner before making it to the hotel. He'd promised to feed his mate, and that was exactly what he planned to do. He slid a hundred-dollar bill across the counter after telling the clerk that Elizabeth was his mate. Fortunately for him, the desk clerk had smelled Rhys' scent when she checked in, or he would have never gotten the key. "Thanks."

He nodded and walked out, jogging up the stairs, not stopping until he reached her door. If he knocked, he stood the chance of her not answering, but if he walked in, the move might set her off. Elizabeth was armed and pissed off, and if he were to just walk in, he'd be taking away her opportunity to choose.

Rhys slid the card key in his pocket before wrapping his knuckles against the door. "Lizzie, let me in."

The door flung open, but his mate kept her hand on the knob, blocking his entrance. Her eyes were red and bloodshot, and the fight she'd shown at his house was etched in the lines of her face. He lifted the bag and drink holder in his hands. "I just came so we could eat together. I promised to feed you. You don't even have to say a word."

She released the door and turned around, walking back into the room. "How did you find me?"

Rhys closed the door and locked it. She had her bag out on the bed, and her hair was wet from a shower. "How about we table that answer until the morning after you've had a good night's sleep."

She turned to him and watched as he pulled the Styrofoam containers out of the bag and set them up at the small table in the room. "Rhys. I can't do this right now."

"Do what? Eat?" He glanced at her as he pulled the lids off of the containers. Her stomach grumbled. "Your stomach says otherwise. Listen, you don't have to say anything. I wasn't kidding when I said we didn't have to talk. I just need to be with you right now. We'll eat and then fall asleep watching mindless television. I promise no funny stuff. I just want to hold you."

He held out a chair for her to sit, but she didn't move. He held his breath as each second ticked by, her hesitation tearing at his heart.

Finally, she gave a little nod and slid into the seat. He breathed a sigh of relief and took the seat across from her, waiting and watching as she picked up her fork. "Thank you for this."

Thank you. He smiled.

****

Elizabeth snuggled into Rhys' warm embrace. His heavy arm was wrapped around her body, holding her tight. He'd been a man of his word, doing nothing more than helping her relax. They'd barely spoken more than a handful of words last night. He'd kept his hands to himself and even offered to sleep on top of the covers as long as she didn't kick him out. She'd opened her eyes to find his blue eyes staring at her, her hand resting on his shirtless chest and her leg entangled with his beneath the sheets.

"Good morning." His husky voice warmed her.

"Morning." She blinked and slowly started to pull her hand away.

He covered her hand and pulled it back to where it was. "I like it there."

She smiled and kept her hand over his beating heart. As much as she'd wished they were together under different circumstances, she couldn't deny there were issues that she needed to address before they could go any further. She didn't even know her own identity, much less what the implications might mean.

"Just two more minutes and then breakfast before we go talk to Jennifer's family." His chest vibrated beneath her hand.

She closed her eyes, enjoying the minutes she had left, where she didn't have to care about anything outside of what was within her four walls.

"I have no idea what's going to happen today." He stroked his fingers through her hair. "But whatever it is, you'll deal with it." He glanced down at her. "You aren't alone anymore, Elizabeth. Never again."

"Rhys, I don't know what the future holds."

"There's time to figure all of that out." He stroked his fingers through her hair. "Let's find the girls first, take down the assholes that are snatching them, and then we'll worry about the rest."

She grinned, glancing up at him. That small statement reminded her that, even though they'd barely known each other two nights ago, he was serious when he'd said that he just wanted to make her happy, because there was nothing else he could have said that would have made her heart beat again with renewed determination.

Elizabeth leaned up on her elbow and over his chest, pressing her lips to his. "I can do that."

Rhys rested his palm on the back of her head but didn't hold her in place. He was letting her take or give what she needed. She held his gaze. "You never did tell me how you found me."

She watched as uncertainty clouded his eyes and knew immediately she wasn't going to like his answer. Sliding out of the bed, she grabbed her clothes and held them clutched to her chest as she waited to hear what he was going to say.

Rhys slid his legs over the edge of the bed and ran his hand through his short hair. "Apparently, Evan can sometimes track you. It's part of that whole thing about you two being connected. When he gave you his blood, he altered more than you being a shifter."

"How so?"

"He made you immortal."

Her mouth parted. He was joking. He had to be. She still walked in sunlight. "Yeah, I'll believe it when I see it. What else did he say?"

Elizabeth's mouth parted as Rhys stood. "He mentioned, before I walked out, that you can block him and that you sometimes already do."

"No wonder you didn't want to tell me

last night." She pressed her lips together, trying hard not to be mad. It wasn't Rhys' fault she had to deal with Evan. "I'll have to practice that," she called out over her shoulder while heading to the bathroom to change and get ready for the day.

An hour later, they'd grabbed a quick bite for breakfast and had just pulled up outside the upscale downtown brownstone in the ritzy part of town. A man dressed in a black trench coat and three-piece suit held a briefcase in hand as he stepped outside the door and turned to lock it behind him.

"Looks like we're right on time," she mumbled beneath her breath and stepped out of the SUV, pulling her badge from her waist. "Shifter Investigation Division. Patrick Smith?"

"Yes."

"I'd like to ask you a few questions."

Mr. Smith turned to look at her. He was in his mid-thirties, with dirty blond hair, blue eyes, and a clean-shaven face. She might even consider him good looking if blonds were her type. They weren't.

"What's this about?" he asked, his gaze going from hers to Rhys and back to settle on her face.

"Jennifer, your missing wife."

He glanced over his shoulder back at the door. "She's not missing."

Rhys and Elizabeth shared a look. She

didn't have to be a mind reader to know he was just as confused as she was by the information. It contradicted what Colton had told her about the newly filed missing persons report on the woman. What the hell was going on?

"Can we speak with her?"

She watched him hesitate, and for a second, she thought they might need to get a court order to talk to her, but he turned back around and unlocked the door. "You can try. She's been sleeping on and off for the last twenty-four hours." He held the door open for them to pass. "Have a seat while I try and wake her."

Neither Rhys nor Elizabeth sat while they waited. She took her time wandering around the living room looking at the wedding pictures out on display, and another picture of the man and the woman Elizabeth recognized from the video feed at the Honey Pot. She was beaming a smile, showing her white teeth in a scene of snow in front of a log cabin.

Their house was immaculate. Everything put in its place. She peeked into the kitchen, not even a dirty coffee cup in the sink.

Minutes later, the woman from the picture took her time coming down the stairs as she tied the red sash to her robe. Her blonde hair was slightly mussed, and she ran a hand down the strands as she hit the last step.

"We're sorry to wake you," Elizabeth said as a greeting.

"No problem. I'm afraid I won't be awake enough to answer your questions until I have some coffee." She continued walking through the room toward the clean kitchen. "Can I get you two anything? What about you, Patrick?"

Patrick followed her into the kitchen and kissed her cheek before answering. "I'm afraid I don't have time. I'm going to be late for my meeting."

She smiled up at him and nodded in understanding before he left.

Elizabeth and Rhys waited until she made a single cup of coffee and doctored it up. She took her first sip and closed her eyes as a moan slid from her lips. "That's what I'm talking about."

She grinned and kept the mug up to her lips. "My husband said you're SID." She glanced up at Rhys. "You're not a cop. You work the bar at the Honey Pot."

Elizabeth pulled her badge. "I am, and he's with me."

"Mmm." She took another sip. "What can I help you with?"

"Are you aware you were reported missing?"

Jennifer stopped drinking and set her mug on the counter. "No."

Elizabeth nodded. "Then I guess you're

not aware that Emily Fisher was murdered and that Sadie and Maria have been possibly abducted?"

"Oh god." She lifted a hand to cover her mouth. "No."

"Mrs. Smith, can you tell us where you went when you left the Honey Pot with your friends two nights ago? We need to establish a timeline and get your alibi."

Elizabeth could tell her words weren't registering with Jennifer. Her face had turned ghostly white, and her were eyes unfocused. She was in a state of shock.

"You look like you're about to faint, Jennifer. Why don't you sit down?" Rhys offered and pulled out a dining room chair.

She sat down in the chair, her eyes glassy as she looked toward the front door. Elizabeth grabbed her mug and placed it on the table in front of her before pulling out the chair next to her.

"Wait...it wasn't two nights ago. I just saw them last night. They can't be missing."

Rhys laid his hand on Elizabeth's shoulder. "That's not possible, Mrs. Smith. Emily was found dead yesterday morning. You were at the Honey Pot two nights ago. Your husband said that you've been sleeping on and off for twenty-four hours. Do you have any idea where you went or what happened when you left the bar?"

She shook her head, a crease forming between her brows as if she was trying hard to remember. "No." She shook her head. "The last thing I remember was us walking in a group to our cars, and then everything after that was black."

"So you have no idea how you got home?"

She rubbed at her temples and closed her eyes. "I don't remember anything." She looked up at them with tears in her eyes. "My friends?"

"We'll find them," Elizabeth said by way of giving her an answer. And she would find them, but in what condition was the question.

"Jennifer, I've already been told you're a shifter. If you don't mind my asking, what's your animal?"

Her brows dipped. "I'm not a shifter. That's crazy. Someone lied to you."

Elizabeth glanced up at Rhys, but neither of them said a word. They didn't have to speak.

"Where does your husband work? We're going to need to talk to him."

"Binks Laboratories."

"Really?" Elizabeth tried to keep the excitement out of her voice. "What does he do there?"

"He's their accountant."

Elizabeth pulled out one of her cards and passed it to Jennifer. "Mrs. Smith, if you don't mind going down to the station and giving our people a sample of your DNA, it will help rule you out as a suspect."

She picked up the card and read it. "Of course, anything to help you find the others. You'll have my full cooperation."

Chapter 12

Elizabeth slid into the passenger seat and dialed the number to the precinct. She waited for the lab to answer and told them she was sending Jennifer there for an analysis. She wanted DNA and to know what shifter strains were showing in her system. Then she had them transfer her to Colton. He answered on the first ring. This wasn't a call she wanted to make, but she had to keep the jerk in the loop.

"I need you to get one of the investigators to work up background information on Jennifer Smith. Her parents' address and numbers and anything or anyone else who can tell me about what type of animal she can shift into."

"You close to finding her?" he asked.

"I did find her, but something is wrong."

"Elizabeth, we should talk about what happened with Evan." She heard the remorse in his voice. Too bad his conscience had kicked in a day too late.

She swallowed around the lump in her throat and kept her resolve. "There's nothing to say unless he told you where the lab is and where the girls are being kept. My resignation still stands. After this one, I'm out. I'll send you my report when I have something new. I just really need that information like yesterday."

"The Jordanian Protectors already have the inside track on this case. His division pulls rank, and they actually want us to fall back. I'm trying to stall them to buy you some time."

"Yeah, well, you can tell Evan that if there is a shred of evidence in what he's said, then I outrank his sorry ass by being the damn princess and I'm not stopping until I bring down whoever and whatever is involved. I'll be waiting for your email, but otherwise, I've got an investigation to run." She paused, taking a deep breath. "Goodbye, Colton."

She hung up the phone, not waiting for his response. What was he going to do, fire her?

"So, now you're their princess?" Rhys asked.

Elizabeth saw the disappointment in his eyes and the way his muscles tensed. He was becoming guarded, and she couldn't blame him. She'd warned him she didn't know what the future held, and that was because it was true. She really didn't.

"It's just a title, one that even I still don't believe, but lucky for me, he does." She started typing notes into her phone. "Bink's Labs and then the senator's residence. He's somehow connected to Emily and Sadie." She glanced his way. "Unless you want to take me to my car. I can finish this alone if you need to go help your brothers at the Honey Pot."

His jaw ticked. Had she hit a nerve?

"I think that might be for the best. Can you take me to my car?"

He looked her way, even more disappointment in his eyes. "I'll take you to your car if you promise to have dinner with me."

"Negotiating?"

"More like compromising." He pulled out onto the road. "I need to check in with the guys and handle the shipment at the bar. After that, I'm free."

She nodded and grinned. She could do compromising. He wasn't trying to rule or run her life. She respected that. "I can compromise."

****

Elizabeth relaxed behind the wheel of her own car and felt alone driving to the lab. Her entire life she'd lived that way. Why it bothered her now, she didn't have a clue. Her first stop was on the outskirts of the Glades, where the lab was located. She parked in front of the building and got out walking up to the rotating doors; she pushed on them and ended up in a large, white, sterile entrance. Waiting areas were scattered around the room with splatters of cheap, fake green trees. She could smell the plastic from the fake leaves as she walked. The open area was void of people, though perfume and cologne scents lingered. A curved welcome desk with two security guards sitting behind it was the only sign that someone actually worked in the building. There were two elevators on her left with a marque hanging on the wall showing a list of names and office numbers.

"Can I help you?" The guard closest to the elevator stood as she approached. She sniffed. Human.

She flashed her badge toward the guard. "I need to speak with Patrick Smith."

He picked up the phone and punched some numbers. "SID needs to speak with Smith."

A couple grunts later and he dropped

the phone back in the cradle. "Have a seat. He'll be down in a minute."

"Thanks." She smiled before heading to the seating area. She stood next to one of the plants with her back to the guards, ignoring the seats that looked about as welcoming, and as comfortable, as sitting on a rock. She gazed out of the floor-to-ceiling window until she heard the elevator ding in the lobby.

She pivoted around to find Patrick Smith strolling her way. He'd ditched the trench coat and suit jacket and was now wearing a white lab coat in its place. He smiled at her, and she sniffed the air, expecting to smell whatever drugs or liquids he'd been using. Instead, she smelled his...fear? *Oh, Mr. Smith, don't you know our kind can smell the stress in your sweat?*

"Detective." He held out his hand in greeting. "I wasn't expecting to see you again. Is everything okay with Jennifer?"

"She's fine." She shook his wet palm and hid her reaction behind the fake smile on her face. Elizabeth gestured to his clothing. "Your wife said you were an accountant."

"Oh, right." He lifted the lab coat. "I spilled something on my suit jacket."

She gave a slow nod. "I just had a few questions for you. You said that Jennifer has been sleeping on and off for twenty-four hours. How did she get home that night after the bar?"

Patrick shoved his hands into his coat pockets. "Jennifer has never been one to handle her liquor. One glass of wine, and she's normally tipsy. When she told me she was going out with the girls, I didn't expect her to come home hammered. Around midnight, when I couldn't reach her on the phone, I got dressed and was heading out to see if I could track her down, but all I had to do was open the door. She was leaning against the railing on our doorstep, passed out. It's amazing she still had her purse and not a single scratch on her car."

"When she woke up, did she say anything to you?"

"She didn't say anything but that she had a bad headache." He ran his hand through his hair. "She took some meds, drank a gallon of water, ate some toast, and went back to bed."

"Thanks for your help clearing that up. Do you know who reported her missing or why?"

"Not a clue." He shook his head and pressed his lips together. "All I can tell you is that it wasn't me."

"Thanks for your time." She patted his arm as she passed heading toward the door, only stopping before she pushed through. "One more thing."

She walked back to him, stopping halfway. "What's your wife's animal?"

"What?" He tilted his head. Fine lines crinkled his forehead. "My wife isn't a shifter."

She sniffed the air as he said the words and got a whiff of what she already knew. He was lying. Why would he lie about something so easy to prove?

He glanced over his shoulder toward the security guards. "If you'll excuse me, I really need to get back."

She smiled and nodded before spinning around and pushing out through the rotating door.

DNA, either in the lab or confirmation by talking to Jennifer's parents, would tell her story. She pulled out her phone and dialed Colton. "Tell me you've got the information on her parents."

"15th and 7th, Lot 22."

She stopped in her tracks. "The trailer park?"

"Yes."

"Huh." She continued walking. "Their daughter lives in the ritzy part of town. I guess I was expecting them to be kind of well off."

"On the marriage license filed two months ago, Jennifer indicated her parents were dead, but when we cross-referenced them in our database, we found them alive and well."

"She is also pretty adamant she's not a shifter, and the funny thing is, she smelled like she was telling the truth. What the hell is going on?"

"She just arrived a few minutes ago to give her DNA sample. I guess we'll know soon enough."

"Copy that. I'm going to talk to the parents. Get the guys to work on finding me someone that has seen this woman shift. Jennifer and Patrick Smith might be denying the existence of her animal, but she couldn't have hidden it for twenty-five years. I need to know what she is."

Colton was saying something into the phone, but she wasn't listening. The hair on the back of her neck stood up as she unlocked the door of her car. She glanced around, letting her gaze scan her surroundings. There was a shift in the air, indicating something foreboding and sinister nearby. She felt it down deep in her core. It felt similar and yet unknown. She felt as though she was being watched and lifted her nose to the air, taking a deep breath. Nothing. She turned back toward the building and scanned the windows to figure out what was causing her unease.

Patrick was standing at a window on the third floor, looking down at her with a scowl on his face. Farther up on the top floor, a man in his fifties stood in the window, also looking down at her. His hands were clasped behind his back. He was wearing a dark business suit that matched his dark hair.

"What do we have here? You're new," she whispered into the phone.

"Elizabeth?" Colton asked with concern in his voice. "Are you all right?"

"If you call two pissed-off men staring down at me from a building all right, then yeah, I'm fine. Listen I've got to go."

She ended the call and palmed her phone. She smiled up at both men and walked back into the building, straight to the marque.

"Detective?"

She waved him off.

The guard picked up the desk phone and was talking in hushed tones as she used her phone and took a picture of the names and floors of the people listed on the marque.

"Thanks, boys," she called over her shoulder and grinned like a kid that had stolen the last cookie. She turned around before pushing through the revolving door. "You can tell them I'll be back." She grinned even bigger as she walked out to her car and glanced up at both windows. The guy in the dark suit had a phone pressed to his ear, looking down at her, but Patrick was nowhere to be seen.

She'd just slid into her car when the

passenger door flew open, and Evan moved into the seat. "You shouldn't have come here."

"Screw you."

He shook his head and pointed out the windshield. "Drive. You're being watched."

She turned the ignition over as she scanned her surroundings. "If you're talking about the guys upstairs, I already know."

"No, I'm referring to a couple of angry wolves."

Elizabeth gripped the wheel tighter as she turned out onto the main street, her gaze going from the rearview mirror to the road and back again. "Stanton?"

"Not him personally, but I think they might be a few of his pack members." He glanced over at her. "Nothing you can't handle. It just seems you're a bit preoccupied lately."

She chuckled. "Yeah, doing my damn job." She glanced back at him and raised her brow. "Which, by the way, I won't cease doing because you insist. You should just go ahead and tell me where the girls are. It will save us both a lot of time."

"Can't do that."

"I should run your ass in and let you sit in a cell. That should change your mind."

He chuckled. "I'd be out within the

hour." He turned to her. "You don't get it, do you? The Jordanians are the reason there is even a Shifters Division in place. We're like the founding fathers. Think of your dad in terms of being like the President. He's the top dog, and referred to as the King of our kind, not necessarily over a continent or some mystical place, but all of our kind, and our existence."

"And I'm the defiant daughter who doesn't follow the rules. Get over yourself. I'm going to find those girls." She pulled the car over and leaned across him to open his door. "And when I do, I'm coming after everyone who could have stepped in to prevent it and didn't."

"You don't know what you're saying." Evan shook his head and slid out of the car. He rested his arm on the door and leaned back in.

"How would I? You've done nothing but keep secrets from me and let me live in a world where I don't belong. Well, guess what. I'm changing all of that, starting with this case."

"Everything that I'm doing...is for you."

"Save it."

"Fine." His lips twitched. "You want answers. I'll give you a glimpse of what we're about. What *you're* about. Meet me tonight at the corner of Cervantes and Fifth." He went to shut the door but paused and leaned back in. "And leave the bear where he belongs."

"As if," she mumbled as the door slammed into place. She watched as Evan jogged toward the tree line. The big sword he'd had strapped to his back yesterday had been replaced by twin katanas with intricate designs. The deadly blades matched the power Evan exuded. He was sexy in a lethal way. The bad-boy type mothers everywhere warned their daughters about. He was the worst. Thoughts of him distracted her from her job, and not in a good way, more of an "I'm ready to strangle you" kind of way.

She put the car into drive again and headed back into the Glades, toward the trailer park. Her mind was trying to put all of the puzzle pieces into place, yet stalling out before she could draw any conclusions. Ten minutes later, she parked in front of a rusted, beat-up trailer in the back of the park against the tree line. The screen door was hanging from the hinges. Old tires and bricks were scattered in the tiny yard. She checked her gun and shoved it back into place before she stepped out of the car. She stood in place and swiveled around on the spot. She felt more eyes on her, yet this wasn't the same feeling she'd had at the lab. She sniffed the air. The unique smells of wolves, cats, and bear were thick in the air as if the property had housed them for years. She glanced at the surrounding trailers calculating who might live where.

Turning, she headed for the door, pulled her badge from her waist, and knocked.

Curses drifted to her ears and grew louder with each step that came closer. An older woman yanked the door open, a cigarette dangling from between her lips. The scent of mildew and mold hit Elizabeth in the face, making her want to hold her breath.

"What do you want?" the woman demanded.

"Are you Matilda Franklin?"

"Who wants to know?" She popped her hip to the side and rested her fisted hand at her waist.

"I'm a detective with SID, and I have some questions about your daughter."

"Jenny? What has she done?" Matilda took the cigarette and flicked the ashes out the door. "I hope you don't expect me to go bail that ungrateful bitch out of jail."

"No, nothing like that. When was the last time you spoke with her?"

Matilda took a drag of the cigarette, and the red embers burned with her pull. "When she was sixteen." The woman turned to walk into the trailer, leaving Elizabeth to follow her. "We had a fight after her first shift. She said she hated us and wished she'd never been born and ran off. We haven't heard from her since."

Elizabeth pulled the door closed as best she could and walked into the dank, dark living room. Dirt covered the windows on the outside, preventing needed sunlight from entering. The couch was torn in a couple of places, the recliner not in any better condition. Ashtrays overflowing with old cigarette butts sat on the tables, and empty vodka bottles sat on the counter.

"You said it was after her first shift? What's her animal?"

"She's a fox."

Elizabeth nodded and let the information sink in. "Do you have any pictures of Jenny?"

"Yeah." She walked over to the fridge and slid a picture from behind a magnet. "She may be a bitch, but she's our bitch."

Elizabeth stared down at the picture of the young blonde with crooked teeth. The only resemblance between the woman she'd met earlier, and the unruly teen in the picture, was her striking blue eyes and the unmistakable mole on her neck. "Do you mind if I hold on to this?"

Matilda hesitated. "That's the only one we have."

"I'll make a copy and have the original returned within the hour."

"Yeah, I guess that would be okay."

"Thanks for your time." Elizabeth gave

the woman a sad smile. She was a mother who missed her child, no matter what the circumstances. Elizabeth felt the waves of sorrow coming from the woman.

"If you see our Jenny..." the woman started to say, her eyes hopeful. "Tell her we never moved in hopes she'd come home."

Chapter 13

Elizabeth stepped down the rickety wooden stairs and over to the passenger side of her car to put the picture on the seat. Her keys slipped free from her fingers after pulling them out of her pocket. She bent down to pick them up and heard the whizzing sound of a bullet splitting the air before the shattering of her window. Glass rained down on her head, slicing her cheek before she could cover her head with her arms. Small shards lay embedded in her skin as she yanked the gun from her ankle holster and trained it over the hood of her car and into the woods behind her.

She sniffed the air, smelling the same

rancid animal scents she had when she'd arrived. She stayed crouched on the ground as the door to the trailer burst open.

Matilda glanced at her. "You all right?"

"Yeah, go back inside and stay low," Elizabeth urged, never taking her eyes from the tree line. She saw the glint of a silver gun poking out from behind a thicket of bushes, and instinctively she knew the asshole was about to fire again. She rose slightly to get the shot, aimed and pulled her trigger seconds before pain sliced her shoulder. The impact thrust her body back into the dirt. "Son of a bitch."

She sniffed, smelling the tangy scent of blood in the air, a mixture of hers and the shooter's. The heavy scent of a wolf was nearby. She heard the cracking of branches moving farther away as the shooter tried to flee. She'd hit him. "You better run."

She tossed the picture into her car through the shattered glass, not wanting to ruin it with her blood. Using her good hand to dial Trapp, she jogged toward the tree line. Blood seeped into her shirt where the bullet had hit her. Blood from the arm, where the glass pieces were embedded, dripped from her elbow as she held the phone to her ear. "Trapp, I'm at the trailer park. I've been hit, and I need the damn trackers."

"Is the bullet still in you?"

She used her good hand and touched the back of her shoulder. Her fingers came away sticky with blood. "No."

"Shift, so you can heal."

"I can't. I have shards of glass embedded in my arms."

"Fuck, Lizzie. Sit tight. Do not give chase. Do you hear me?"

She ended the call, shoved the phone in her pocket, and held her arm as she jogged toward the trees where she'd seen the glint of the gun. She slowed to a walk, scanning the area as she entered. She smelled the musky scent of the wolf that had been there. Surprisingly, the scent was unfamiliar. She was unable to put a name to the stink. She just couldn't catch a break today. She'd expected to smell Horace's unique odor, yet it wasn't his. She followed her nose toward the smell of gunpowder, and she spotted blood on an outcrop of leaves. She grinned through the pain. "You're as good as mine."

Ten minutes later the entire trailer park was surrounded with units, along with Dr. Jamieson Tanner, the division's personal doc. He walked straight to her while the others worked on canvassing the area. She was sitting on Matilda's dilapidated steps when he reached her. He eyed the bullet wound, dressing it immediately. "Let's get this glass out of you so you can shift and heal."

"That sounds like a good idea, Doc," Evan added, appearing by her side. "Was it the wolf?"

"Yeah, but it wasn't Horace." She glanced up at him as Jamieson started pulling stuff out of his bag. "Why are you here?"

"I was already on my way before I got the call. I sensed you were in trouble."

"We should do this in my office," Jamieson announced.

Elizabeth stood and walked over to her car. She opened the passenger door, reached in, and grabbed the picture that Matilda had given her before turning and tossing her keys in the air to Evan. "Do you mind?"

"Your wish is my command."

"If that were true, my case would be solved, and you'd be gone." Elizabeth rolled her eyes and followed Jamieson to his car, not waiting on a smart-ass reply from Evan.

Fifteen minutes later, she was sitting in the doc's office, watching him use a magnifying glass and a pair of tweezers as he tried to pry the glass from her flesh as if they were splinters from a tree. He eased a sliver out and dropped it into the metal bowl on the table next to him.

"Jamieson, do you have family?"

"No. My parents died a long time ago,

and I was an only child."

"Someone special in your life?"

He smiled as he continued to dig glass out of her arm. "I don't have time for a social life with the way you guys are always getting hurt."

He dropped another sliver into the bowl and dropped his smile. "Jennifer Smith, the woman you sent for testing, came by earlier."

"That's good." Elizabeth sucked in a deep breath when Jamieson started digging deeper near her elbow. "What animal is she?"

He stopped poking, glanced up at her, and frowned. "She doesn't have one. She had some anomalies in her DNA, but no sign of any animal."

"You're serious?" Elizabeth's mouth parted. "That's not possible. Her own mother told me she was a fox. Did you check that gene?"

He shrugged and started digging again. "I'll run it again just to be sure."

"Thanks."

"By the way, when you ran my blood work back when Colton first brought me in, did you see anything to indicate that the enzymes in my bite or the secretions in my blood had the potential to kill?"

Ping. He dropped another larger glass piece into the container.

"Well...Trapp mentioned you can shift

into any animal, and if that's possible, then yes." He shrugged. "Even if you only do a partial shift, if your psyche chose something with a poisonous bite, then I can see how you could kill."

"What about if I meet a mate and I'm bitten? Is there a chance I could have poison in my DNA? Are there any animals that are poisonous if eaten?"

He pushed back from her, picked up his tweezers and the bowl, and walked across the room to the sink where he sat them down. "Let me think about that."

He pulled open the separator that some of his patients used to change clothes behind and gestured for her to get behind it. "You need to shift to close the wounds."

She stepped around the curtain and started undressing. She heard him clicking away on his computer as she tossed her shirt and bra over the screen before stepping out of her shoes and ditching her jeans and panties.

"Giant Namibian bullfrog," he called out.

She peeked around the screen. "Excuse me?"

"Poisonous secretions in the skin of that type of bullfrog can cause kidney failure and death if not cooked right." He pointed to the screen and kept scrolling as she pulled off her socks. "However..."

She peeked back around. "Yeah?"

"Wood absorbs the poison." He gestured toward the computer. "According to this, when chefs cook the bullfrogs, they line the bottom of the pots with wood to absorb the secreted poison."

"And people eat them?" She shivered at the thought while making a gagging sound.

"Not only do they eat them, they are considered a delicacy."

"With that DNA in your system, you could potentially be deadly. You'd kill the human and their animal."

She concentrated on a little white fluffy cat as she shifted, letting the magic take over. Her bones cracked and pushed and pulled into place, fur sprouted from her arms, and her fangs pushed through her gums. She looked down at her paws expecting to see white fur and was aggravated when she saw the brown and orange paws of the Siberian tiger again.

She stepped out on all fours from behind the curtain and glanced around the room. The doctor was still sitting in front of the computer, but his chair was turned and looking at her.

"That's a fine, scary animal, Lizzie."

She purred and walked closer, rubbing up against his leg. She used her head and nudged his hand, lifting it to the keyboard.

"You still want me to keep searching?"

She purred again and kept walking around the room. Within seconds, her skin was healed, and she felt like a hundred percent.

"All better I see," Evan called out as he walked into the room.

She hissed at him, giving him a good look at her deadly incisors before sauntering back behind the curtain and letting the shift overcome her again, putting her back into her human state.

She ran her fingertips across the new tiny pink scars on her arms before looking at her shoulder. If she kept up this line of work, her body was going to be one big pink mess of scars. She reached for her panties and started getting dressed again. When she was done, she stepped around the partition, moving to stand behind the doctor. She placed her palm on his shoulder as he continued to click away at the computer.

"Keep looking for me, Doc. It's kind of important. And let me know what you get after rechecking the DNA." She laid the picture of Jennifer down next to his computer. "Can you have one of the guys make a copy of this and have it delivered back to Jennifer's mother tonight at the trailer park? I've got some assholes to find and bite." She chomped at the air and grinned.

"Sure." He stopped typing and glanced

up at her. "I'll call you if I find anything out."

"What is he looking for?" Evan asked as he followed her out of the room.

"He's doing some research for me. Where's my car?"

"Getting fixed. I'm afraid you're stuck with me tonight."

She glanced to the front doors of the precinct, and her eyes widened. She'd lost track of time, spending more time in the lab getting glass pulled from her than she'd thought.

"You need to take me back to my hotel. I have a date."

"With the bear?"

"With my mate," she clarified as she reached for her phone, realizing too late that she didn't have Rhys' number programmed in her phone. She glanced toward Colton's office to find the light off. "Where's Colton?"

"He shifted to hunt with the trackers."

She let out a long deep sigh and started for the door. When he didn't follow, she turned around. "Well, are you my ride, or am I calling a cab?"

He gritted his teeth as he stormed toward her. "Do you know how much it pains me to drive you to see *him*?"

"Fine, I'll call a cab," she announced and picked up the phone on the nearest desk.

"Get your ass in gear. I'm not waiting all night," he grumbled and gave a violent push out the door.

Lizzie climbed into the passenger side of the SUV and buckled her belt as Evan started the SUV and pulled out onto the main road. She was stuck with him for the next thirty minutes. "I appreciate the ride."

He grunted.

"Maybe I can meet you tomorrow night for that glimpse of Jordanians you were going to give me. I'm kind of beat tonight and just want to enjoy a late dinner with Rhys."

He glanced at her but didn't say a word. His fingers tightened on the steering wheel. Minutes went by before he spoke. "Elizabeth, you're wasting your time with him." He glanced over at her again. "You are too different."

"Opposites attract."

He shook his head and let out a long sigh. "If you won't stop seeing him for yourself, at least think about what you're depriving him of."

"Yeah, what's that? Because I haven't heard him complain yet."

"Children," Evan answered without looking at her. "A full mate bond. You'll kill him if he bites you."

Elizabeth rested her head against the seat. "He'd love me without those things."

"Your father will never accept him."

She balled her fists, digging her nails into her palms. "You mean the same father who didn't want to raise me and sent me to live with his brother among humans? I can't say I honestly care about what he thinks."

"You don't, but what about Rhys? Your father is a powerful man and shifter. What if he turns on Rhys and his brothers? We have laws, Ab—Elizabeth. His laws and the laws of your bloodline have governed our people and kept us alive for centuries. What happens when the king decides that Rhys isn't good enough for you? Will you condemn Rhys and his brothers to whatever punishment your dad sees fit?"

She shifted in her seat to get a better look at Evan. "Are you sure you aren't saying this because you're jealous, and you want me as a mate?"

"No." His voice lowered. "I'm telling you this because I care about you. I always have. It killed me to wait for you until you turned twenty-five." He glanced at her, and his brows dipped. "I know you, better than you know yourself. If something were to happen to him, you'd never be able to live with yourself. You'll either get yourself killed trying to rescue him or get him killed. Mates or not, neither you nor I can let that happen."

She turned back in her seat without

another word and watched the darkness pass by as she let his words sink in. She'd lived most of her life alone, so it was possible she could walk away if it meant that it kept him alive, even if it destroyed her happiness, but there had to be another way for them to be together. For them to be happy.

"Someone once told me that a shifter's number one priority is to protect and take care of his mate. That her happiness always came first." She glanced sideways at him. "That's how I know you and I aren't mates. We might be connected by destiny and lives, but you'd never walk away if I begged you to, even if it meant that I'd be happy, truly happy, whereas Rhys would if it meant my happiness. As much as it would kill him, he'd let me go."

She turned and rested her head against the window for the remainder of the quiet ride back to her hotel. The night grew darker as he turned into the hotel and parked. He got out and followed her upstairs no matter how much she protested that he get back in the car and leave.

The door swung open, and her bear's gaze softened as it rested on her face. He pulled her into his arms and glared at Evan. "What is he doing here?"

"She was shot, and one of us had to take care of her," Evan announced before turning to walk away.

"Asshole," she called out after him.

He lifted up the car keys, keeping his back to her as he walked away. "Takes one to know one, Abigail."

Chapter 14

"I hate that guy," Rhys grumbled, shutting the door and locking it.

"Join the club."

"You were shot?" Rhys' brow creased with worry as he stroked her arms in a gentle caress. His eyes swirled gray, and his jaw hardened. Concern radiated from him in waves, and his sincerity caused her pulse to quicken.

She laid a gentle palm on his face, waiting for his hardened jaw to loosen and his eyes to turn back to the vibrant blue she loved. "I'm fine."

He let out a deep breath, his hold stayed gentle on her skin. "Where were you hit?"

She pointed to her shoulder.

He reached for the hem of her shirt, lifted it over her head, and tossed it onto the bed. He eased the strap of her bra down over her shoulder before lightly running his thumb over the fresh pink mark. He leaned down and pressed his lips to the spot, showering it with slow caresses from his lips.

"Where else?"

She lifted her arms, and he traced his fingers over the angry marks before he eased her to sit down on the bed. He knelt in front of her and kissed a path up one arm and down the other. His tenderness toward her injuries, and his mouth on her skin ignited a fire in her veins. The sensual yet caring way he was treating her was unlike anything she'd ever experienced. His unfamiliar response made her heart soar and confused her at the same time.

"Where else?"

She unhooked her bra and tossed it on top of her shirt. Running a finger between her breasts, she teased, "Here."

His lips quirked at the sight of her creamy flesh. There were no pink marks, but he was getting the picture. Inching her back on the bed, he climbed up her body, holding himself over her. He smiled up at her as he leaned in and licked a path from her navel up to her neck, where he pressed another kiss. He cupped her breast as he ground himself between her legs, letting her feel just what waited for her behind his zipper.

"Rhys."

"Hmm?" He kissed a path up the side of her neck, stopping right below her ear.

"You can't bite me." She turned her head to look into his eyes. "Promise me you'll never bite me."

He eased off of her, sliding to the side but keeping a possessive hand splayed on her stomach while resting his cheek in his palm. "Why not? Is it because of Evan and what he said? Because I don't give a shit what he says. You're mine, Lizzie. I've known it from our first kiss, and I know you feel it, too."

He moved his fingers to rest beneath the snap of her jeans and her skin. He was inches away from where she wanted him to be, but she knew the minute he touched her between her thighs, all rational thought would float away.

"Biting me could kill you, and I won't take that chance. Not with you, not ever." She turned to face him, cupping his cheek. "And I won't bite you. I can't. Not if there is a remote chance that I can hurt you. We can never have a full mate bond." She swallowed around the lump in her throat, knowing her words were upsetting him. Better to get it out in the open now than in the heat of the moment, when she might have to fight off his damn bear.

Rhys rolled onto his back and laid his arm over his eyes. "Why are you doing this? Do you have feelings for him?"

"Damn it, Rhys." She slid off the bed and grabbed her bra and shirt and clutched them to her chest. "I'm telling you because I want to be honest with you. It wouldn't be fair for me to keep that information from you. I like you. I like us, and as far as feelings for Evan go, yeah, I do have some, but it's not the same. I might not understand our connection, but he isn't my mate."

"Damn right, he's not." Rhys moved his arm and glanced at her. His face was unreadable as he slid from the bed, stalking toward her. He slipped the clothes from her hands and tossed them back on the bed. "I am."

He popped the buttons on her jeans and slowly undressed her, taking his time and running his fingers down the outside of her legs and up her inner thighs, touching every inch of her except for where she needed him most. Goosebumps on her skin contradicted the fire raging in her veins. The erotic anticipation left her wet and wanting.

He stood up in front of her and began removing his clothes at a lot faster pace.

"Are you wet for me, Lizzie?"

Her breath quickened as he ditched his jeans, his erection and desire evident. She reached for him, wanting, needing to touch him. She stroked his silky shaft, rubbing her thumb over his bulbous head.

He clicked his tongue and moved her hands out of the way, pulling her closer. He spun her, pressing her back to his chest, the warmth of his body surrounding her. His hands rested possessively on her naked body. He cupped her breast with one hand, rubbing her nipple between his fingers until it pebbled, shooting a line of fire down to her clit. She moaned, resting her head back against his chest. His other hand rested on her belly, slowly moving down between her thighs.

He used his leg and inched her stance farther apart.

He kissed her neck as he held her tight. "I'm going to make you come with my fingers," he whispered in her ear. He pressed another kiss to the sensitive juncture on her neck, licking her flesh. A haze of desire clouded her eyes. "Then with my mouth." He continued to tease as he rolled her nipple tighter between his fingers. "Only then will I give you my cock."

She moaned louder at his erotic promises, leaning into his touch. She was wet and wanting just from his words as she tried to lift her hips to position his fingers where she wanted them. Where she needed them.

"What are you waiting for?" she baited him, her words coming out a whisper.

He slid his fingers easily through her curls and into her folds. She rewarded him, grinding her ass against his erection.

"You are wet," he said as he ran his teeth over her neck. She stiffened in his hold. "Don't worry, baby. I'm not going to bite you." He pressed a kiss to the scratch he'd left. "Not yet."

"Never," she whispered, her own words clouded with desire.

He shoved a finger inside of her, working first one and then another. Her channel contracted and clenched him, trying to suck him in deeper. The welcome sensation drove her closer toward release. He increased his thrusts, using his other hand to hold her open and rub against her heat. She closed her eyes and let the feelings wash over her.

"That's it, Lizzie. I want to taste you on my fingers."

Her channel tightened, every nerve ending on fire.

"Come for me, baby."

She clenched her eyes closed. Her toes curled as she fought going over the edge.

"Give it to me, Elizabeth. It's mine," he growled in her ear before rubbing his thumb over her clit in hard small presses.

Lights flickered behind her closed eyes, and a moan slipped her lips. Her body convulsed as her climax hit. Her legs grew so weak she might fall if he released her.

He slowed his fingers, riding her through the first wave.

"Ready for round two?" he teased, slipping his fingers free and sucking them into his mouth. He turned her and pressed a hot kiss to her lips, letting her taste herself on his tongue.

"How about we skip to round three?" she teased.

"Not a chance," he answered. He eased her toward the bed, where he made good on the rest of all three promises, four if she counted him taking her in the shower when she was trying to get clean.

After ordering room service and eating, they lay nude and exhausted under the covers, her resting in the crook of his arm with her leg tossed over his. Her palm rested on his chest; she enjoyed the content rhythm of his heartbeat beneath her fingertips.

"I meant what I said," she announced into the quiet room. "You'll never be able to bite me. Are you okay with that?"

"We'll work it out," he answered.

"Rhys." She stroked a circle on his chest. "I still don't know anything about my future. This could get complicated."

"You're my future, Elizabeth. That's all I need to know. There's nothing we can't handle together." He pulled her closer and stroked her hair. "Now get some sleep so we can go find these assholes. I want to be able to take you home so we can start our life together."

"I gave Colton my resignation," she whispered.

"Then you'll be able to follow your passion."

"What if it's catching bad guys?" She turned to face him. "What if it's working for the Protectors?"

His eyes caressed her face as if he were carefully deciding how to answer her question. "Then I'll buy you a sword."

She grinned. "What if it's ruling like my father?"

"Then I'll buy you a crown."

She leaned up and pressed her lips to his.

"What if I just want to be your wife?"

"Then I'll buy you a ring."

She rested her head back in his embrace. "What if I want all three?"

"As long as you're happy, I'll always support you, no matter what you decide."

"What if it means having to let me go?"

He stroked her hair and remained quiet. Leaning in, he kissed her forehead. "Get some rest."

****

Elizabeth leaned back into the SUV's leather seats as Rhys drove toward the senator's residence. She pulled up her pictures to get a better look at the names on the lab's marque.

"Whatcha looking at?" Rhys asked as he glanced her way.

"I went by Bink's, the lab where Patrick Smith works so I could ask him some questions about Jennifer, and when I left yesterday, I noticed Patrick and another man higher up in the building watching me from the windows. Neither of them looked too happy that I was there."

"Did you ever find out what animal she has?"

"According to her husband and her DNA, she's not a shifter." Elizabeth pulled up her camera and turned her phone on Rhys, snapping his photo to save in her phone. She smiled.

"Really?" he asked in disbelief.

"Yeah, but according to her mother, she was a fox."

"Was, being the key word." He glanced over at her. "Do you think she was injected with a modified version of the same serum that Evan claims would have killed you and your animals?"

Her head snapped up, and she turned to look at him. "I blew up the entire lab and took out most of those guys. Do you think they started the program up again?"

"Probably, and not only that, but it looks like they perfected the drug."

She clenched her eyes closed and shook her head. "I knew I should have tracked those last two bastards down to the ends of the earth and killed them. Damn it. I'm so fucking stupid."

Rhys' fingers closed around her hand. "My mate isn't stupid."

She opened her eyes to find him staring at her.

"My mate is sexy and smart, and I have all of the confidence in the world that you'll save those women and see this through to the end."

She gave him a small smile. *Even if it kills me.* She kept that thought to herself.

They arrived at the three-story mansion on the hill and parked in the circular drive. The white house was enhanced with ornate columns along the front. The shrubs and grounds were perfectly manicured, evidence her tax dollars paying his salary were hard at work.

"How do you know he's home?"

"I called his office while you were getting dressed. They told me he was on vacation."

"Okay." He got out of the SUV and waited around in front for her. "What exactly does a senator do when he's on vacation?"

She shrugged. "I don't know, but we're about to find out."

She jogged up the concrete steps to the double wooden doors and rang the bell. A few seconds later, a maid in full uniform answered. "Can I help you?"

She flashed her badge and a genuine smile. "I'm Elizabeth Hanson, and I'd like to speak with the senator, please."

"Is he expecting you?" the maid asked.

"No."

She gave a slight nod but opened the door farther to let them in the entryway. "He's in a meeting, but if you'll wait here, I'll tell him that you're waiting."

"Thanks." Elizabeth watched the woman walk on silent feet over to a pair of double doors.

She opened them wide, giving Elizabeth a great view of the senator standing behind his desk. He had on a pair of blinding, god-awful bright yellow and pink plaid pants and a white polo. He looked as if he were about to go play golf and wanted to make sure anyone on the course could see him coming from a mile away so he wouldn't get hit with the tiny ball. Two other men in business suits sat across from him, with their backs toward the door.

The maid whispered into Senator

Hayes ear, and he lifted his gaze at her. The smile he'd had on his face slipped, and Rhys moved closer to her, resting his hand on her lower back in a possessive fashion.

Hayes pasted a smile on his face until the maid walked out, shutting the doors behind her. "He'll be with you in a few minutes. If you'd like, I can show you to the library."

"No, thank you; we don't mind waiting here." There was no way in hell the maid was moving them away from the spot. She wasn't about to miss seeing who the senator was meeting with while on vacation.

The maid scurried off, leaving them in the hallway outside the office.

Rhys leaned down and whispered in her ear. "Did you smell them?"

"No, did you?"

"Oh, yeah. You're going to love this." Rhys pressed his lips together in a smirk, biting back the smile on his face.

Seconds later, the door opened, and all three men piled out into the entryway.

The senator was the first through the door, followed by the man who had been watching her from the top floor of the lab. His eyes narrowed, but he didn't say a word. Behind them, Evan strolled out. *Surprise, surprise.* She grinned at the confusion on his face. Yeah, she was getting close. His presence confirmed it. His eyes met hers before flicking to Rhys and back to hers. His brow creased before he masked his surprise and gave them a curt nod in passing toward the front door that the senator was holding open.

Duck and run. Elizabeth grinned.

The senator followed them out, closing the door behind him. She could hear their loud whispers but couldn't make out their words. She debated moving toward the door, but Rhys placed his palm on her arm and stopped her. He gave her a small shake of the head. "You can ask later."

"You can bet your sweet a— Senator." She smiled in greeting as he walked back inside.

"Detective. I hope I didn't keep you waiting long."

"Not at all." She grinned as he held out his arm toward his office to guide them inside.

Before the senator shut the door, a little girl squealed as she ran down the hall. "Daddy, Daddy," she called out after him, running as fast as her little legs would carry her. She was dressed in a swimsuit with her hair up in pigtails, holding an inner tube around her waist.

"Rebecca." He knelt down to the little girl's level and caught her before she slipped on the pool water running off her feet. "What did I tell you about running in the house?"

"But..." She pointed back down the hall. "Cousin Brandon threw me into the pool, and I almost drownded. He called me a big baby and said I was a natural swimmer and I shouldn't be scared."

The senator's eyes grew wide as he glanced their way. "If you'll excuse me a minute."

They nodded and waited for the senator to walk off.

"Did you smell her?" Elizabeth leaned over and asked Rhys.

"Hard to mistake the smell of a baby bear cub. Do you think she's adopted?"

Elizabeth shrugged and glanced at the picture on the desk. The senator was with a woman wearing a hospital gown, holding a little baby in her arms while he was beaming, smiling down at both of them.

"I'm so sorry about that." The senator walked back into the room and shut the door. "We shouldn't have any more interruptions."

"She's adorable," Elizabeth said, pointing toward the photo on his desk.

"She can be." He grinned. "She's kept me and her mother on our toes since the day she was born."

Elizabeth could feel Rhys glance her way, but she didn't look at him. She already knew the question going through his mind because it was rolling through hers. The shifter gene was, in most cases, passed down through the male's DNA. She sniffed the air confirming her suspicions. The Senator was as human as they came. The fact the kid was a shifter, and her dad wasn't, meant that his wife had an affair. Did he know? Was he even aware that was how it worked? Or had he, like Jennifer, killed his animal, too?

"We didn't mean to interrupt your meeting earlier. We called your office, and they said you were on vacation."

"Don't worry about it. You saved me from a boring meeting with my CEO and some security."

Her brow rose, but she didn't ask any more about it. There was nothing he would tell her that she couldn't get out of Evan later when she kicked his ass.

"What can I do for you?"

"Your name came up in our investigation."

"Oh, yes, I heard. Are you looking into Sadie's disappearance?"

Her lips twitched. "Yes, we were told she works for you. Were you aware that you'd employed a shifter?"

The senator leaned back in his chair and gave her cocky smile. "Yes, I know everyone on my staff. Believe it or not, Detective Hanson..."

Ah, now we're getting somewhere.

"...I don't have any problem with the

shifter community."

Elizabeth sat back in her chair and crossed her legs. "No? Then why are you trying to pass a bill to have them all implanted with microchips? Are you scared of them? Us?" she amended, throwing that little fact back in his face.

"On the contrary." His smirk fell. "It's just as much for their safety as it is for ours. Without some type of log of who is where and what they are, then we'll never be able to treat them if something should happen. If you were to have read my bill, you'd know that it's not about the chip as much as it's about providing them with equal rights to everything. As with our government, regardless of race, color, or creed, we're all accountable for our actions."

"And this chip? Do you just plan to use it for identification and GPS?"

"No," he answered without pretense. "It will also contain a paralyzing serum to disable them from shifting."

"Do you realize how that sounds and how it will be affecting the rights of all shifters?"

He leaned forward and crossed his arms on his desk. "What happens if a shifter goes on a killing spree? How do you suppose we track him and stop him?"

"How do we stop a human from doing the same thing? You call the police, and in this case..." She sat back in her chair. "You'd call us."

"And in the event that it's organized crime? More than one, hell, more than you have on your force. How do we stop them then?"

She tilted her head. "And just who does your bill suppose holds the remote to stop us when we get out of line? You?"

The senator narrowed his eyes. "A third party, justice department board, of course, comprised of shifters and humans. I hired Sadie, not based on what she shifted into but based on what type of job she did. I don't discriminate, Mrs. Hanson."

His eyes flicked from hers to Rhys' and back. "Now, if you'd like to schedule time to debate my bill, you can set that up with my office. If you've come to ask questions about Sadie's employment, then I suggest you stay focused and on task."

Elizabeth held in her anger and re-crossed her legs. "Are you aware that Emily Fisher was found murdered?"

"Should I know who that is?" he asked.

She could smell the deceit from across the room. She refrained from calling him a moron, knowing that if she did, she'd get kicked out.

"She was an attorney at Kleinfield and Summers."

His eyes quickly narrowed before he

masked his frustration. "Is there a question?"

"She was working on a case for you the night of her disappearance. Do you mind telling me what it was about? It would save me time from having to subpoena the records."

He rose from behind his desk. "You're going to do it anyway, aren't you?"

She grinned and rose, too.

"This meeting is over. Any other questions can be asked through my attorney."

She chuckled and headed to the door, followed by Rhys.

"Afraid that's impossible." She glanced back over her shoulder. "Emily is dead. Which partner are you using now?"

"Get out," he growled.

"With pleasure," she answered back as she opened the door. "Oh, one more thing." She turned to face him. "Are you aware shifters can smell when you're lying?"

His nostrils flared, but he didn't say anything.

"Rebecca is a pretty girl. Funny thing, she doesn't take after you or your wife."

The senator balled his fists when Rhys ushered her out of the room and toward the front door.

"I'll have your job," the man called after her.

She gave a full belly laugh and turned around walking backward as Rhys continued to drag her out of the house. "I've already turned in my resignation, but I have every intention of finding Sadie first." She winked, before turning and strolling out of the door. "You can count on it."

Chapter 15

Rhys waited until Elizabeth was in the car and they'd pulled out of the driveway before he spoke. He'd tempered his reaction because he wanted to support her in this endeavor, but damn it, she was going to get herself killed.

"Do you realize who you've just pissed off?" He glanced her way, the grip on the wheel tightening as he tried to control his bear clawing just below the surface. He'd wanted to roar with pride at the way she'd stood up for herself, but on the other hand, he wanted to throw her over his shoulder and get her the hell out of there before she put a bigger bull's-eye on her back. Shit.

"A crappy politician that doesn't deserve to be in office," she answered matter-of-factly before glancing out of the passenger window.

"But he *is* in office." He glanced at her.

"I know his secret. He won't come after me."

"Dead people can't tell secrets. He might not personally come after you, but you knowing his secret is exactly why he will."

She let out a long sigh as she turned toward him. "I'm not here to make friends, Rhys. I'm here to find the missing girls."

"Yeah?" he answered sarcastically. "And how is that working out for you? You're alienating everyone you're talking to. You already have more than one target on your back. How many more, baby, before you start to take this shit seriously?"

She snapped her gaze to his. "I want justice."

"For who? The girls? Or for what happened to you in the past? Or maybe from the father who gave you to his brother to raise? Did you see a little bit of your situation in Rebecca? You have a lot of anger to deal with, baby."

He reached over, trying to hold her hand, but she yanked it away, balling her fingers into a tight fist and resting it in her lap.

"Lizzie, I care about you. You are my mate, and it's my job to protect you and make you happy, but right now I don't know how to do either."

He pulled the car over onto the side of the road and put it in park before he turned to her. "Tell me how to fix your anger and take away your pain. Just tell me, and I'll do it."

Her angry eyes watered as she turned away from him to stare out the window again. He was starting to understand her, even if she didn't understand herself. She had two tactics when people pissed her off, two different reactions. She either withdrew by running away or turned into a ticking time bomb set to explode. Fuck. He ran a hand through his hair.

She needed help, and as much as it pained him to think it, she needed more than he could give her.

He got out of the SUV, rounded to her side, and pulled her door open. He unhooked her belt and pulled her into his arms. She was stiff beneath his touch, her face was red and blotchy, and it was a miracle she hadn't shifted into something that could beat his bear's ass or eat him.

"I'm sorry." He used the crook of his finger to raise her chin to look at him. Her watery eyes stared back at him, cutting his anger off. "I'm just worried about you, Lizzie. I've just found you, and I'm not ready to lose you."

He was a dick. A mate didn't talk to the woman they were falling for like a total prick, but he couldn't seem to stop himself. At the rate he was going, she'd dump his butt and go to Evan, and what would he say to stop her? Beg for her to forgive him? Sometimes the truth was painful and even harder to bear coming from someone you cared about, but it needed to be said. After how she'd come back to the hotel last night, and after what he'd just witnessed, he was amazed her strong-headed ass was still alive. Shit.

She looked up at him with sadness in her eyes, and his gut clenched tight. He'd caused that look, and he was ready to kick his own ass because he was the one person who was never supposed to hurt her.

"I'm not perfect, Rhys. I never claimed to be. If those girls are going through what I went through..." She closed her eyes, dropped her head and gave it a little shake. "I have to find them," she said with more conviction. "And more than that, I have to find what's driving these assholes to continue. If I just knew, I could stop it. I could stop them from hurting anyone else." She glanced up at him. "I have to stop them."

He wrapped his arms around her, holding her tight. He kissed her hair, unwilling to let her go. "You're a survivor, baby. No one can take that away from you. Not the guys who abducted you, not the senator, not any of the shifters that want you dead, not even your father or Evan. You've survived all of this time without their help, without mine." He leaned back to look down at her face. "You will catch these guys. I just need to know that you *will* live through this because if you don't....it *will* destroy me."

She relaxed into his arms, and he felt some of her anger dissipating with each breath. He leaned down and pressed a kiss to her lips before releasing her and tapping her on her fine butt. "Come on. We have work to do," he announced as he rounded the car, slid back inside and waited for her to shut her door. "Let's review. So what do we know for sure?"

"Emily Fisher is dead; Sadie and Maria are missing; Jennifer was reported missing, yet she wasn't."

"Who reported her?" he asked.

"No one is taking credit for it, so I'll have to review the tapes to see when it was called in."

He gave a slow nod. "What else do we know?"

"Jennifer hated her fox, but her DNA was somehow altered."

"Okay, and no one is taking credit for that little surprise, but we have to be looking for the mastermind behind that alteration. What else?"

"Evan is neck deep in this crap and was meeting with the senator and the guy I saw at the lab who was scowling at me from the top floor."

"Okay." He glanced at her. "Let's take each one separate."

"The senator has a bill up for passing that is going to piss off a lot of shifters. He's also the father of a cub that isn't his, which might be why he's involved."

"I don't follow."

She shrugged. "A man trying to hide a secret, especially when he'll be running for re-election? Maybe he wanted to hide the proof that his wife cheated on him."

"I'll work that angle." He slid his fingers through hers. "Drunks tend to talk...a lot. I'll ask around and see what I can find out from the bar and some of the shifters in the Glade. They might be more willing to talk to me than you since I don't carry a badge."

She turned to him and smiled. "You'd do that for me?"

"Of course." He lifted her fingers to his lips and kissed the inside of her palm. "So now you know what you need to check into. The missing person report, background on the people at the lab, and the man who was meeting with the senator."

He pulled into a parking space in the SID lot and turned off the ignition. He turned to her. "I need you to trust me."

She tilted her head. "You're the only person I do trust."

He gave a slow, knowing nod. "You might not like what I have planned, but I need you to know that I'd never hurt you."

"What are you talking about?"

"Nothing to worry about." He leaned over and kissed her lips. "Meet me at the bar later."

She held his face and pulled him in for another kiss, letting her lips linger against his. "Okay." She opened the door and was about to get out when he stopped her and placed his SUV keys into her hands. "You're going to need wheels." He winked. "I'll call Max to come get me. He should still be in town." He leaned in once more and kissed her. "Watch your back, Lizzie. They're gunning for you."

She gave him a mock salute. "Yes, sir."

She got out of the car and met him around the back. She clicked the lock button with his fob and leaned up, resting her arms around his neck. She pulled him down and pressed a tender kiss to his lips. "You're not half bad at being a mate."

He grinned. "Is that your way of saying you approve?"

She chuckled as she turned to walk off, and he smacked her ass.

I hope she still thinks so after tonight. Rhys pulled his phone out of his pocket and called Max to come pick him up. He hung up and then dialed the one man who was sure to help. "Cousin, you owe me, and I'm calling in my favor."

He walked toward the road and paced the lot. "I want you or one of your guys to follow her today if she leaves the building."

"She's not going to be happy," Colton argued.

"She may not be happy, but she'll be alive. I also need you to text me her number and Evan's."

"Why do you need to talk to Evan?"

"It doesn't matter why. I just need this." He ran a hand through his hair. "Lizzie needs this."

"Fine, I hope you're right."

He hoped his plan was the right thing to do too. His life and his mate's happiness hung in the balance. Rhys hung up the phone and waited for the text. He took a deep breath, trying to loosen his shoulders. He dialed the number and waited for Evan to answer.

"What the fuck are you trying to do, get her killed?" Evan growled in greeting, keeping his voice low

"We need to talk. Be at the bar in an hour."

"I'm in the middle of something."

"If you really want to help her, then be

there. She needs something only you can give her." Rhys shook his head, not believing that he'd just said those words and disconnected the call. He texted Elizabeth with his number and grinned when she texted him back with a heart.

****

Elizabeth sauntered into the dispatch room and straight up to the supervising department head. Mark smiled up at her, guided her into his office, and shut the door.

"Well, this is a pleasant surprise, Hanson. What brings you to my little corner of the world?"

"My case." She took a seat across from his desk. "Someone reported a woman missing, and she wasn't. I need to know who called in the report, and I figured coming straight to the top would streamline my efforts."

"Depends on how the report was given to us." He tilted his head. "All of our audio is recorded, so if it was an anonymous caller, you'd be able to hear the person's voice, but they probably wouldn't have given a name. If it was called in by a relative, they'd have given us the information, or...they could have just come into the office to file the report, which means you'd be able to see exactly who it is on our security cameras." He poised his hands above his computer keyboard and waited. "Let's take a look. Who's your missing person?"

"Jennifer Smith. Someone reported her missing four days ago; the same day we were notified about the death of Emily Fisher."

His brow rose. "Two women?"

"Actually, four."

"It may take a few minutes to get you the exact information." He started clicking away, and his brows dipped in concentration.

Elizabeth leaned forward, resting her elbows on his desk as she watched him work.

"Jennifer Smith was called in at three-twenty in the morning." A few more clicks, and he turned up the speakers in his computer. A crackling sound came to life.

"911, what's your emergency?"

"Jennifer Smith has been kidnapped," a familiar male voice said.

"Sir, what's your name?"

Elizabeth leaned closer, closing her eyes to make sure she was hearing him correctly.

"My name is of no concern," the caller said. "You need to find Mrs. Smith. Her life is in danger."

Her brows dipped as she opened her eyes. Her heart dropped into the pit of her stomach. She knew that voice as well as she knew her own. It hit her like a ton of bricks in the chest. Evan had made the call, but why was a question only he'd be able to answer. "Can you send me a copy of that audio clip?"

"Sure." A few clicks later, and it arrived at her phone.

He continued pounding on the keyboard as she got up to leave. He glanced up at her, "Don't you want to know who called in Mrs. Fisher's death?"

"Absolutely." She eased back down into the chair.

He hit play and leaned back in his chair. "Oh god, send an ambulance to 15th Street. She's dying." A woman panted into the phone as if she was out of breath. "He promised to turn her, and he killed her, and now he's going to come after me."

The phone disconnected, and Mark met her gaze. "Does she sound familiar?"

Elizabeth shook her head slowly. "Play it back."

Matt hit play again, and Elizabeth closed her eyes to see if she recognized the voice or could pick up anything else in the background besides the woman's heavy pants. She leaned in closer to the computer. In the background, she heard what sounded like a car door slam closed before the phone clicked off.

She opened her eyes. "Can you send

me that one, too?"

A few clicks later, and that one arrived at her phone. "Anything else I can do for you, Elizabeth?"

"No. Thanks for your help." She gave him a kind nod and left the office, more confused than when she'd arrived. The woman had to be one of Emily's friends, yet she could rule out Jennifer. She'd heard her voice and knew her lies. It wasn't Jennifer who had called in Emily's death. No, this woman was scared, and from the sound of it, running.

Elizabeth stopped by her desk, pulled a couple of paralyzing darts from her drawer, and eased them into her pocket. After checking the clip in her gun, she shoved it back into the chamber and stuffed it in the back of her jeans. A copy of the school picture of Jennifer as the gangly sixteen-year-old with the crooked teeth caught her eye, and she grabbed it, too. She stared down into the girl's blue gaze before sliding it in her other back pocket. She headed toward the doors and stepped out of the office, lifting her face up toward the afternoon sun. The warm caress was a gentle reminder she'd lived another day. Rhys was right about one thing. She was a survivor, and today wasn't going to be any different.

Sliding behind the wheel of the SUV, Elizabeth tried to process the woman's phone call she'd just listened to. Her heavy pants, the shutting of a door.

Elizabeth drove to the ritzy part of town. She knocked on the door of the ritzy brownstone. She needed answers and knew exactly where to get them.

Jennifer pulled the door open. She looked better. The color had returned to her face, not to mention that she was much more awake and dressed for the day.

"Detective?"

"Mrs. Smith." Elizabeth smiled. "I have a couple more questions for you."

"Sure." She stepped back, allowing Elizabeth to enter her house.

The house was quiet. The smell of coffee clung in the air as she stopped in the living room. Elizabeth pulled out her phone and pulled up the sound bite of the woman's phone call. "Do you recognize this voice?"

She hit play.

The color in Jennifer's cheeks drained, and her eyes bulged as she listened to the frightened woman. "Yes," she whispered. "That's Maria."

Elizabeth nodded. That's who she'd thought the caller might be, but she'd still needed validation.

"Thanks." Elizabeth didn't hesitate to pull out the picture of Jennifer when she'd been sixteen. "And this is you?"

Jennifer pressed her lips together and narrowed her eyes, unable to mask her surprise. "Where did you get that?"

"Your mother." Elizabeth sighed. "What happened to your fox?"

Jennifer's shoulders deflated, and she dropped her gaze. "No one was supposed to know." She looked up, her eyes begging Elizabeth to understand. "He hates shifters. He never would have married me if he'd known."

"Jennifer, what did you do?"

Jennifer sat down on the couch and rested her head in her palms. "I never asked to be a shifter." She looked up as a tear slipped from her eyes. "I only ever wanted to be normal."

Elizabeth shoved the picture back in her pocket.

"What did you do?" Elizabeth asked again with a bit more authority, knowing that Jennifer's answer was important.

Jennifer cleared her throat. "When I found out I was an animal, I ran away from my parents. It was their fault I'd never be normal." She rose from her spot on the couch. "I lived on the streets for years, just barely surviving while I searched for a cure, anything that would make the fox go away."

Jennifer lifted her chin. "I met a man." She shook her head. "He said he could help me. He said that he'd already helped others just like me."

"And you believed him?"

"Detective, I was on the verge of suicide, ready to end my own life. You don't know what it's like to get picked on for being the runt of the group. When you add in that I'm a fox, that knowledge just made things worse. So, yes...I believed him."

"And he killed the fox?"

Another wet tear slipped down over her cheek. "Yes." Her words came out a whisper.

"How?"

She didn't answer.

"Jennifer, I need to know how he did it."

"He gave me an injection."

"What did it do?" Elizabeth softened her voice.

"I didn't think it worked at first. I was lying on a bed with an IV hooked in my arm. He pushed the liquid in, and it wasn't until about fifteen minutes later when I felt the effect. I screamed in agony. My insides were on fire; I felt like I was dying, and then I blacked out. That was all I remembered." Jennifer visibly swallowed. "He killed the fox inside of me that day, and I've silently mourned every day since."

Fresh tears slid down her cheeks before she cupped her face. Her shoulders trembled with her silent sobs.

"Jennifer." Elizabeth laid her palm on her arm. "I need to know the man's name. Who did this to you?"

She swiped at her tears and grabbed a tissue to blow her nose. "I never knew his name. He never told me. Everyone on the street just called him Raw."

"Will you meet with a sketch artist at my office?"

She started shaking her head quickly, and fear struck her eyes. "No, no, no. I can't let my husband find out."

Elizabeth touched her arm in reassurance. "Your husband doesn't need to be involved, but if we can put a face to the name, it might help us find your friends."

"I can't do it now." Her voice trembled. "I'm about to meet him for lunch, but I can come by after."

"That would be great." Elizabeth gave Jennifer's shoulder a gentle squeeze before heading to the door. "I'll call ahead and tell them to be expecting you later today."

Jennifer hugged her waist. "I hope you catch him. I may have asked to kill my fox, but I was only a kid. I didn't know what I was doing."

"We'll find him." Elizabeth gave a slight nod, walked out, and jogged down the steps toward the SUV. She repeated the name to herself as anger swept through her body, "Raw."

Elizabeth drove on autopilot to the alley where they'd found Emily. She parked on a side street and walked to the mouth of the alley and turned in place. The road was mainly deserted with only a few buildings nearby, including the club. A few cars sat in the parking lot but not many. She scanned up and down the street, her mind working to imagine the scene when Maria's call had taken place and where she might have run.

Unable to determine where the woman might have run, Elizabeth walked farther into the alley. The tall, old brick buildings around her blocked the afternoon sun from her eyes, casting dark shadows on the pavement. The stench of rotten food from the dumpsters and cans drifted to her nose. Flies swirled around, attracted by the potential feast. Scanning the ground and everything she passed, she continued walking, looking for something that the crime scene unit could have missed or overlooked. There was nothing.

As she reached the end of the alley, Elizabeth shielded her eyes from the sun and scanned the small street where delivery drivers could park to offload shipments. Beyond the asphalt was an open field leading to an outcrop of trees that ran the length of the entire block. The trees were the outer edge of the jogging path that circled the nearby park. "This is where she ran."

She sniffed the air and smelled Colton before she saw him. She spun around to find him leaning against a brick wall in the alley. "I was wondering how long it was going to take before you realized I was behind you."

"What are you doing here?" she asked, frozen.

"Same thing you are." He shrugged and straightened. "Looking to see if we missed anything." He stepped up beside her. They scanned the same trees she'd been looking at.

"I listened to the 911 calls. The woman that called in about Emily was running as she made the call. She was out of breath." Lizzie nodded toward the trees. "Care to take a walk?"

Colton smiled. "I thought you'd never ask."

There was an awkward silence between them as they crossed the open field. Colton spoke first. "I should have told you about Evan."

"Yep." She continued walking beside him. "You're half human." She gave him a sideways glance and grinned. "You're allowed to make a mistake or two. Just don't let it happen again. Not when it's something important, like that."

She bumped his shoulder, and he bumped her back, making her giggle for the first time in a long time. She loved Colton like a brother, and while she'd been angry at him, it made her feel as though a part of her was missing. He was not only her boss but also her friend; the only friend she'd had for a long time, and giving that up wasn't something she could easily accept. He'd screwed up, but they all did. It was an inevitable part of life.

She loved Colton like a friend, nothing compared to the love she felt for Rhys. Her eyes widened, and she tripped over her own feet, righting herself before she fell.

She couldn't love Rhys? It was too soon. No. She pushed the thought aside.

"What's the matter? Forget how to walk?"

She gave him a little shove with her hand. "Hardly."

They walked slowly through the trees, stopping to check anything that looked remotely out of place. A few soda cans and trash was all they found. Colton rested his palm on her arm, stopping her from taking another step. He inhaled a deep breath sniffing the air, prompting her to do the same. A very faint scent of wolf drifted to her nose. When she opened her eyes, she could see the pack of wolves in the distance. They were coming at them from all angles. She glanced behind her. The street was free and clear.

"What the...."

Colton spun her around the nearest tree and pulled her to a crouch. "Shift or run?"

She peeked back out from the tree and still hadn't spotted the one wolf that was the bane of her existence. The only wolf brave enough to threaten her. Horace was nowhere to be seen. "I'm going to shift." She placed a hand on his arm. "There's too many of them for you. You need to go back."

"Like hell." He growled and rose, tearing off his clothes.

She jumped up from the spot and hurried to remove hers. If they were going to fight, she needed whatever advantage she could get.

She let the magic take her over, feeling its pull and push over her body. Her teeth lengthened and sharpened, yet her body didn't shift. She felt stronger and sharper than any of her other animals. Her vision turned red.

"Shift," he growled as if waiting for her to take her form.

"I did," she replied and looked down at her human arms. "The only thing that changed was my vision...and I feel stronger."

"Evan," he whispered. Grabbing her arms, he swung her around to face him. "Lizzie, you're immortal like a vampire. He should have told you, but we don't have time to argue. Your body is recognizing your vampire traits. You're fast, and your strength will break bones. They won't see you coming."

"No." She shook her head. "That's not possible."

He lowered his head to meet her gaze. "He bit you and willed you to survive because he's dead. He imposed his will for you to live because he could. He has a direct link to you."

"They aren't real," she argued back, yanking her arms free. "I don't drink blood, and what about the sun?"

"I don't have time to explain. Just trust me." He glanced back around the tree. "Shit. Twenty yards and closing."

He took her arm again. "He can hear you if you call to him in your mind. That's how he knows when you're in trouble. You've been doing it all along."

Within seconds, Colton shifted into his grizzly and lifted to stand on his hind legs. His roar shook the ground, pulling her back into the coming fight.

"I'm going to kill you, Evan," she screamed in her mind, hoping to hell that she gave the asshole a headache.

Elizabeth balled her fist when the first wolf took flight, jumping to attack Colton head-on. She sprang into a run and caught him mid-air, squeezing his mid-section. She heard his bones crack before she tossed him to the side. Fast was an understatement. She'd barely just blinked and had the wolf between her arms. Her strength rivaled that of her dragon, and better yet, she had arms instead of wings. She didn't see the downside of being a vamp, at least not yet.

The others snarled, the saliva dripping from sharp teeth as they paced, looking for an opening to attack. She watched them, keeping her back to Colton. They wouldn't get to him, not if she had anything to say about it.

In a choreographed move, all five of the assholes but one jumped on her at once. Mouths clamped down on her skin as she yanked one away, throwing it into a tree, and the rest were tearing at her skin. She screamed. Using all of her strength to yank and pull, breaking two of the mutt's jaws, she tossed them aside. Blood covered her body, oozing from her wounds. Her strength was failing, and she fell to her knees, and that's when she saw Horace step out in his wolf form from behind the nearest tree. His yellow eyes glared at her, his snout shaped into a growl, giving her a menacing glimpse of his fangs. He leapt at her at the same time as the others, and Colton barreled into him, swatting him to the ground.

Chapter 16

Max parked the truck right next to Dylan's in front of the club. They weren't opening for another five hours.

"You doing inventory today?" Max asked Rhys.

"That and I have to make some calls. Elizabeth needs me to look into a few things."

"Where is your new mate? Did you seal the deal, or did she run again?"

"She's still looking for the missing girls." He pulled the door open to the club. Dylan was behind the bar, wiping down the bar to unstack the glasses ready to be put away, along with the new bottles of liquor to add to the shelf.

The door flew open behind them. Evan's eyes were glowing bright red, and his teeth were extended. He looked like one of the monsters in a fairytale his mom used to read him as a child.

"What the..."

"Abigail's in trouble." Rhys heard a bear's loud roar, followed by howls on the wind. The afternoon air was filled with screams.

"Where is she?" Rhys demanded, knowing she was close enough for him to hear Colton's anger.

Another ear-piercing scream.

Evan's eyes turned pure white, void of pupils as he spoke. "She's near the park."

He blinked, and the red glow returned to his eyes, glowing in anger. "She's losing blood. We have to help her."

Rhys didn't wait on the others as he tore through the building, bursting out the back. Fire fueled his anger. Lizzie was hurt. Whoever had dared lay a hand on her was about to die. Spotting them just inside the tree line, he ran, pumping his arms and legs as fast as they would take them. He shifted in mid stride. His clothes shredding into pieces as he landed on paws instead of feet as he crashed through the tree line. He growled, smacking at the wolves on his mate. He'd knocked three of them off when another one jumped. He caught him and broke his neck, tossing him to the side.

He stood in front of Elizabeth, blocking her. Colton was next to him, bleeding from his fight. His brothers took up places on each side, forming a semi-circle around her, growling and daring any of the wolves still standing to try again. He roared, and they inched back. Four bears versus the three wolves left standing and the two wounded. It wouldn't take much to finish them off.

Rhys heard Elizabeth moan in pain. It was the only thing that kept him from chasing the others that were running off. He turned to find Evan lifting her in his arms. His bear growled as Evan started carrying her back to the bar.

"I'm the only one that can help her." He looked over at Rhys as Rhys began the shift. "No offense, big guy, but if she takes your blood, you'll die, and then she'll really kill me."

Evan pushed through the back door of the club and into the security room with the big tables.

Elizabeth lay limp in Evan's arms as he eased her down onto the table in the lounge area. She turned on her side, gripping her stomach, moaning in agony.

"Elizabeth." Evan's voice was deep and calming. "Look at me," he compelled, and she turned to face him.

"You feel no pain." He brushed the hair out of her face, and her moaning stopped. Holding his arm to his mouth, he ripped it open before holding it to her lips. "Drink."

She latched on, holding his arm with both hands. Rhys watched her eyes close.

"How is this possible?" he whispered.

"We need to leave." Evan pulled his arm free, and Elizabeth's eyes opened wide, and she hissed with her pointy teeth. "We need to leave now."

He placed his hand on her forehead. "Sleep, Abigail, sleep."

Rhys watched in amazement as her eyes fluttered closed and her body went limp.

"Why did you do that?" Rhys yelled, his bear wanting to break free.

Evan scooped her up in his arms. "Because she needs more blood than I have, and if she tried to drink you, it would kill you." Evan glanced up at him. "If she bites you, then you'll die. Not that I would mind, but she'd kill me. I need to take her to the others. Together, we can help her, but we can't here. Everyone's at risk. Get dressed, bear. You're coming with us."

Colton came jogging into the room. "Horace is dead. The rest took off."

"Where are her damn shots?" Evan questioned.

"I don't know. She was given plenty to

pack for this trip."

Rhys stormed into his office and grabbed another pair of clothes, shoving his legs into his jeans. He pulled a shirt over his head and carried his shoes with him.

"What shots?"

"They're specially designed just for her. They mask her scent with an added kick of the blood enzyme that sustains us. That's why she never knew she was immortal."

Evan carried her toward the front door. Max tossed Rhys his keys as he stormed by. "Where to?"

"The compound," was Evan's only answer.

****

Elizabeth fought to open her heavy lids. Loud, angry voices pulled her from the dark, deep sleep that had consumed her. She rolled her head, and her whole body ached. Her muscles were stiff and heavy to move. Where was she? Dead? Or worse, had Horace captured her?

The yelling in the room stopped, giving her a reprieve from her pounding head.

"Lizzie." She heard Rhys calling her name, felt his touch on her forehead. "Everything is going to be okay, baby. It's time to wake up."

She tried to speak, but her words came out in a moan as she turned her head into the warmth of his touch.

Her eyes slid open, and she blinked until she could focus.

She heard Evan's command. "Rhys, you need to step back. We don't know if we gave her enough."

"Fuck off," Rhys growled back. His lips felt familiar and warm on her hand.

"Rhys." She croaked his name. Each syllable felt like tiny shards of glass cutting and ripping her dry throat.

"I'm here, baby." He lifted her into his arms, cradling her head. "You need to drink this."

He pressed it to her lips, and she opened for him, grateful for the cold liquid that replaced the fire and pain. The liquid was sweet and tangy, unlike anything she'd ever drunk. The color was dark red, but she didn't care.

He set the glass down and eased her back down on the pillow.

"Where am I?"

Memories started to flood her mind. The fight? Colton? The wolves? She gasped and tried to push herself up as fear gripped her heart and squeezed tight. "We have to help Colton."

"He's fine, Lizzie." Rhys picked up her hand and kissed it again.

"Where am I?" she asked, turning her

head to look. The lights in the room were dim. No windows on the wall. She tried to move her hand, but Rhys stopped her. She turned toward her arm and saw the IV stuck into her vein.

"Rhys?" Her voice rose an octave, laced with panic.

Evan answered from across the room. "You're at the compound, Elizabeth."

She turned toward his voice to find him leaning against the wall, his arms crossed over his chest, and he was wearing the familiar scowl that she'd come to know.

"What compound?" she asked.

"Our base of operations. It was the only place we could treat you."

"I don't understand." She turned her questioning gaze to Rhys, and he shook his head, closing his eyes in resignation.

"You needed our enzymes to survive. Without them, you would have died or ended up killing whoever was around you," Evan answered.

"Way to sugarcoat it, asshole." Rhys turned to growl at Evan.

Evan stepped closer. "She needs to know, and I take full responsibility. I should have taught her how to fight the immortal way."

"Wha..." Memories of her shift into a vampire flashed in her mind. Her eyes narrowed as she turned to him. "You! You did this to me."

He remained quiet, unspeaking as he watched her.

The door to the room flew open, and a big brooding man stepped inside. His salt and pepper hair was cut short and matched the color of the stubble on his face. It was a face she recognized instantly. Twins, she remembered Evan telling her. This man was her father. The same asshole that had sent her away to be raised by his mortal brother.

"Everyone out," he demanded.

She felt the power rolling off of him and pulsing in the room. Evan walked out of the room without question. Rhys didn't budge, remaining firmly by her side.

Elizabeth swallowed and leaned back against the pillow. Did she really have to do this now?

"Out now."

She snapped her gaze to the old man. "Rhys stays." She glared at him, daring him to tell her and Rhys what to do. "He stays, or you and I won't be discussing anything."

Her father's jaw ticked, and his eyes were calculating. He might look like the man who'd raised her, but she could see the cold look behind his eyes. "You don't have a say in this, Abigail."

Elizabeth yanked the needle from her arm and tossed it on the other side of the bed. She eased herself up; using what strength she had, she slid her legs over the side of the bed. "My name is not Abigail. It's Elizabeth, but then you wouldn't know that, would you? You don't get to tell me what to do. You gave up that right when you tossed me out like the trash to be raised by your brother."

Rhys helped her stand, keeping her steady with an arm around her waist, supporting her as her vision clouded and swayed.

"Elizabeth." Her father's voice softened. "Fine, he can stay." He gestured back to the bed. "Now sit down before you fall."

Elizabeth didn't follow his orders. If she sat back down, she wouldn't be getting back up again and depending on what dear old dad had to say...she might still be leaving.

"You can be angry with me, but I did what was best for you. Please..." He gestured to the bed.

Lizzie eased down to sit on the bed, keeping hold of Rhys' hand.

"That's a hard sell, old man. How was it best I didn't know I could shift? It might have saved my life. Or, more importantly, how was it best for me when I was abducted?" She rose from the bed again, and anger stirred in her belly. "Was it best that I didn't know how to defend myself? Was it best that I can shift into all kinds of animals, including one that will never let me experience my mate's bite? Explain that."

"Elizabeth."

She watched her father's patience dwindling, as he grew tired of her tirade, and yet she didn't care. Irritation flashed behind his eyes. Good, because she was pissed, too.

"Everything you went you through and everything you are has turned you into a stronger woman that will one day rule in my place."

She shook her head. "You should have had more kids. Maybe one of them would want the job."

Her thirst returned with a vengeance. Her throat constricted, and she felt the length of her pointy teeth protruding. She squeezed Rhys' arm and closed her eyes. *Evan, you better get your ass in here and fix me,* she grumbled in her head, angry at herself, angry at her father, and angry at the man who'd turned her into this monster she didn't know how to control.

"Elizabeth, what's wrong?" Rhys asked while helping her lie back down.

"She hasn't had enough enzymes," the man claiming to be her father said as the room started to spin out of focus.

Evan burst through the door and rounded the bed. He picked up the IV and shoved it into her vein before lifting the cup she'd been sipping from back up to her mouth. She took a long pull, only stopping to gulp some air.

"She needs more, and you're not helping." He glanced over at her father. "She needs rest, sir. This conversation needs to wait." Evan bowed his head out of respect. "Please have one of the other guards show Rhys his room."

"I'm not leaving her."

Elizabeth reached for his hand and squeezed. "I'll be fine." She shook her head and gave him a small smile before turning to look at her father. "Rhys is my mate. If anything happens to him, you should know that I'll tear this place apart brick by brick with everyone in it." She narrowed her eyes in challenge. The room flashed red, and she knew that one of her beasts was seconds away from bursting free and out of control.

"You, my dear, were born to be a queen." Her father grinned and gave her a slight nod as if he'd approved of her demanding, threatening outburst before escorting Rhys from the room.

"Asshole," she grumbled as Evan propped more pillows behind her head and handed her another full glass of what she'd been drinking. He pulled up a chair and leaned comfortably back, crossing his legs at the ankles.

"You know what they say about the

apple and the tree." Evan grinned while lacing his fingers behind his head.

"What the hell am I drinking?" she asked, looking down into the cup. It looked god-awful no matter how good it tasted. If she ever got in a similar predicament and knew how to take care of it herself, she wouldn't have to rely on anyone else, least of all these people. She wouldn't be coming back to this place.

"It's a blood and enzyme concoction. It's the way our kind receives nutrients without having to eat directly from the source."

"The source being anyone with a vein?"

"Yes." He let out a long sigh. "You especially can't bite others because you'd kill them."

"Why do I need this now when I didn't before?" she asked and began sipping again.

"We had it stored in the shot you were taking to mask your scent."

Elizabeth covered her mouth to stop from spewing her drink everywhere. "Jamieson knew?"

"Jamieson is the head and lead physician of the Protectors. He's one of ours, strategically placed into your world to see to any and all of your medical needs."

Another man she considered a friend was what...working for her father? Her heart cracked a little more.

"It's not what you think, Abigail."

"Elizabeth," she corrected him. "And it's exactly what I think."

"Jamieson is like us. He's an immortal. He delivered your grandfather, your father, and then you. He's an important part of your family and the ONLY person I trusted to see to your needs when I couldn't bring you in."

She shifted her gaze to his. "You wanted to bring me...here?"

"Of course. This is where you were to return when you turned twenty-five, although it was to rule under your father, but after giving you my blood, I always knew you were destined to become a protector." Evan uncrossed his legs and sat up, resting his elbows on his knees. "I need to train you how to fight and teach you how to use your new skills. You are one of us, Elizabeth. You belong with us, living among us, and fighting beside us. It's who we are. It's who you are. I know you better than you know yourself. The throne will never make you happy, not like fighting to protect the innocent people of the world."

"My whole life was nothing more than an elaborate lie. Is Rhys even my mate, or is he part of this world, too? Did you guys give me some bad juju full of pheromones to make me feel that pull?"

"Hardly," Evan answered and stood up, walking to the other side of the bed where the empty IV bag hung. He began replacing it with a fresh bag before sitting down on the side of the bed, leaving one foot on the floor. "Tell me what you want, Elizabeth. What will make you happy?" His haunted eyes held hers. She felt the sorrow, his feelings and knew that he genuinely cared.

"I want to find the girls. I want to destroy the lab and protect the other shifters from asinine laws meant to restrict them. I want to feel the mate bond with Rhys without killing him. I want people to quit withholding the truth from me because they don't think I can handle it. I want..." She let her words trail off. "It doesn't matter what I want. You guys have manipulated my entire life."

He took her hand in his. She felt the strength in his touch, the support he offered. "You shall have all of those things and more."

She looked up to meet his gaze.

"Get some rest, Elizabeth." He patted her hand. "Once you're better, we'll start on that list of yours. Rest assured, I know for a fact the women being held are fine, and we will rescue them."

He rose from the bed and walked to the door. Pulling it open, he paused. "I'll check on Rhys to make sure he's comfortable and then start planning the rest. You have my word, not as your protector but as the other half of your soul. It will be done."

He bowed as if addressing royalty and walked out of the room, leaving her with nothing more than her thoughts.

Chapter 17

Two weeks later, Elizabeth lay sprawled on her back on the sparring mat. Sweat beaded her brow, and her chest rose and fell from her deep breaths.

"You won't win lying down," Evan called to her from the other side of the mat, resting his hands on the hilt of his sword.

"Give her a break," Rhys argued with his arms crossed over his chest as he leaned against the wall. He looked at her and smiled giving her the push she needed to ignore her sore muscles and get back up.

"You're fighting with human constraints. Only you are not human,

Elizabeth," Evan said while lifting his sword and moving around the room as though he was preparing to attack again. "You are immortal."

She flipped to her feet, slicing the air with her katana.

"You are faster than any animal in your body. You can control minds and bend wills to do your bidding." He advanced on her, bringing his sword down in an arc.

She caught his sword with the katana and pushed him away, narrowing her eyes.

"Attack," he ordered. His voice deepened as his impatience grew with each step as he circled her.

She ignored him, devising a plan in her mind. Evan was right about her speed, about her ability. She'd practiced, and she knew her limits, but she also knew the worth of having the element of surprise on her side.

"When I best you, and I will,"—she grinned—"then my training is done?"

One of his brows rose in challenge. "If you think it's possible, give it your best shot."

Keeping a straight face, she followed his movement, each step and slice of his blade. He was watching and waiting, preparing to strike with a predator's grace.

"Evan, where were you when I was

five?"

His brows dipped being caught off guard at her question, and she stifled her smile, not giving him an inch of understanding.

"I was learning to wield my first sword," he answered.

"Do you know what I was doing?" She grinned and ran toward him. When his sword came down toward her, she dropped her sword and grabbed her dagger from the sheath at her waist. Using her immense speed and control, she somersaulted from the mat into a double flip over his head, landing behind him. She tilted his head to the side, the sharp point of the dagger pointed at his neck.

"I was in gymnastics," she breathed into his ear, "perfecting that move." Lowering her weapon, she stepped back. "You don't know everything about me, much less my desire to get the hell out of this room and back to work. We're wasting time."

"Well done, Abigail," the king called out from the other end of the room where he was standing just inside the doorway.

"Elizabeth," all three of them answered back in unison.

Rhys tossed her a towel before handing her a bottle of water. He'd been so patient with her during their time at the compound. His brothers had taken over his role at the bar so that he could help her work things out. His life was on pause while hers was finally starting to take shape. Finally starting to feel as though it meant something and where she might actually fit in, not as a princess or even a queen or even the old man's royal daughter but as a protector. When she'd met the others, the tension between them was thick. Having trained with half of them, proving herself capable in combat, they'd let their guards down and treated her just like another guardian and not the spoiled princess they'd assumed her to be.

Her relationship with the old man was courteous at best. She ignored his attempts to make amends, keeping him at arm's length and not giving him the affection he was after, not wanting to risk another heartbreak when he didn't return her love. It was easier that way. They might be related by blood, but the affection stopped there. To her, he was no more than another man who had let her down. Another man who had thrust her into a world that had almost killed her.

"Meeting room in five minutes," her dear old dad announced before disappearing from the room.

Rhys pulled her into his arms for a sweaty kiss as Evan hooked the weapons back onto the wall.

"I talked to Max. The senator's wife lost

her mate in a fight before she ever met the senator," he whispered into her ear. "When the Senator and she married, she was already pregnant and still grieving."

Elizabeth's mouth parted. "You're sure?"

Rhys shrugged. "That's the rumor."

Rhys tossed his arm around her shoulders, and they followed Evan out of the room and into the conference room. Rhys walked in behind her, his hand on her back when one of the guards they'd nicknamed Striker stopped him with a hand on his chest.

"This is a private meeting."

Rhys growled and narrowed his eyes at the bastard. How dare he try to keep Rhys out of the conversation? If he wasn't allowed, then she had no desire to hear what the mighty king had to say.

Elizabeth moved to stand beside him and knocked Striker's hand off Rhys' chest. "You will not talk to my mate that way."

Silence fell over the room, everyone in attendance turned and glanced in their direction, waiting and watching the exchange like an oncoming storm.

Striker's eyes narrowed, and he tried to intimidate her by closing the distance. *Bring it on, asshole.*

"I wouldn't do that if I were you," Evan called from the other side of the room where he'd already taken his seat, his feet propped up, his fingers laced behind his head. "She can kick your ass."

"She? Hell, I can do it myself," Rhys growled and grabbed Striker's hand in a grip that he couldn't break.

"Striker," her father grumbled in the silent room.

Rhys released Striker's hand, giving him a little shove. If anything, it was as if he bowed his chest in contempt, ready to throw down.

Oh, try me, asshole. I'll tear your balls off and fry them with my dragon.

"Dude, stand down. She's ready to shish kabob your balls over a flame." Evan chuckled. "She can do it, too."

"Get out of my head, asshole," Elizabeth growled while returning Striker's challenging gaze.

His lips twitched as he stepped back, giving them the royal nod as she and Rhys passed, taking seats at the opposite end of the table from where her father sat.

"It's time we take the lab." He winked in her direction as if he was doing her a favor. She'd take it with or without his help. He turned toward Evan. "What's the status?"

"If you've known where it is all along, why have you waited? You're letting innocent women die."

"No one being held has died," Evan

assured her and pushing back his chair he stood. "The situation has shifted. The man running the operation is like a ghost, and rumor has it he's due to visit in the next forty-eight hours, in order to move the facility. Something has changed to bring this man out of hiding. My men on the inside have kept the women safe thus far, thwarting the scientist's efforts at the lab at every available opportunity and keeping their animals safe, yet sedated." He glanced her way before continuing. "But they've started packing up equipment, and an order has been passed down that they won't be taking their prisoners with them."

"Where are they?" she whispered. She'd take the damn place herself if the plans changed. There was no way she was letting them kill the women. Not after everything she'd been through. She'd die trying if she had to.

"In a warehouse, a mile north of town."

Elizabeth's hackles rose. Anger rippled beneath her skin. The room flashed into a red tint. Rhys rested a hand on her leg, the only thing keeping her calm. He gave a slight squeeze as if reading her mind. She glanced at him and took a deep, calming breath before the red haze disappeared.

"The senator agrees that it's time to move."

Elizabeth snapped her gaze back to

Evan's. "He's not in on it? I was certain..."

"No." Her father was the person to answer. "Because of his daughter and his wife, they have just as much at stake in this venture as we do."

"Huh, a man that cares about his daughter. Wonder what that's like," she mumbled beneath her breath. The senator cared more about his illegitimate child than Elizabeth's father had cared about her.

Elizabeth leaned back in her seat, pondering what the hell that meant. She'd been sure the senator was behind everything the way he'd been pushing implants and his bill. She was positive he'd wanted to use the mysterious drug on his child to hide her paternity. It was the only logical conclusion....not that his intent was to want the instigators stopped.

"And the man from Binks?" she asked, glancing up at Evan. If she'd been wrong about the senator, was it possible she was wrong about him, too?

"The operatives we have positioned inside have been supplying him with the liquid they'd planned to use, in the hope his lab could produce an antidote in the event our guys couldn't save everyone."

Elizabeth rubbed her temples. How could she have been so wrong?

"And Jennifer Smith?" she asked, glancing up at Evan. "You called in her disappearance."

"It was a tactical move. We're still trying to figure out her involvement," her dad answered.

"DNA testing confirms her fox was killed. She doesn't have an animal anymore." Elizabeth leaned forward, resting her elbows on the table. "She said she doesn't want her husband to know. He hates shifters."

Evan retook his seat. "Did she tell you who injected her? I've had the records checked. She's never been at the lab on the outskirts of town."

"A guy that goes by the street name Raw. Jennifer didn't know his real name. Do you think he's the one we're after?" A shiver of fear trickled down her spine. "Do you think there's more than one lab?"

"Makes sense," Striker added. "None of our operatives have seen the real man running the show."

"Who do they take their orders from?" Rhys asked.

"A man they only know as the General," Evan answered.

"How does the General keep everyone from rebelling? I mean, he's surrounded by armed guys and has shifters working for him to abduct others of their kind. How is it he calls the shots, and no one has challenged him, and why haven't our operatives used mind control?"

"We believe he's an immortal," her father answered. "They are the only ones strong enough to control the minds of others and use a barrier when our men try it on them. It's the only thing that makes sense."

She glanced around the table. "I thought we were the only ones. Are you telling me there are not only more out there but that they're rogues?"

Evan dropped his gaze to his lap. His lips pressed together as if he was afraid or embarrassed to answer her questions.

"We should discuss this in private," the king answered quietly.

Elizabeth heard Evan's voice in her mind. *Your mother.*

"What about my mother?" Elizabeth asked.

The king turned his glare at Evan.

"What? She has the right to know. No more secrets, sir."

Her father's face turned bright red with anger as he slammed his fist down. He rose from his position, standing at his full height. "Your mother had a lover, and she turned him so that they could run away together."

"Oh, for crying out loud." Elizabeth threw her hands up and stood. "Is my entire family dysfunctional with a crazy gene? Surely there is a normal strand in our past somewhere." She crossed her arms over her chest.

"You would be wise to be mindful of your words, daughter."

"Yeah, well maybe you should look up the definition of that word, *Father*." She glared at him. "I thought she was dead. You guys don't even speak of her. Where is she? What happened to her?"

"She was dead the day she betrayed me," her father answered, holding her gaze. "Her lover killed her with a stake through the heart and then burned her body until there was nothing left but ashes."

"That suggests she was immortal." She glanced around the table. "Who turned her if it wasn't my father?"

The table remained silent, and no one answered. She wasn't sure she'd ever find out that answer, if they didn't come clean with the information.

Her heart crumbled again. Damn, another person she'd never have the opportunity to ask why she'd been given away.

The king stormed over to the door and yanked it open, glancing back. "Evan, we're storming the compound in twenty-four hours. Warn your operatives. There is no way this son of a bitch survives. Do you understand?"

Evan gave a royal nod.

****

Elizabeth laid in Rhys' arms in their temporary accommodations at the compound, nestled away on remote acres of land away the city. She'd barely shut and locked the door before they were stripping off clothes and reaching for each other. He needed her as much as she needed him. Two hours and a shower later, they lay quietly in the bed. Her hand rested over his heart, her mind replaying everything she'd learned today.

"Get some rest, Lizzie." He kissed the top of her head and pulled her closer. "We're going to have a long day tomorrow."

She glanced up at him, her heart breaking. She hadn't had the nerve to tell him that he wasn't going. There was no way she'd risk his life, not when there was a mad man that could get inside of Rhys' mind and take control. She'd argued with Evan in her mind, and yet she knew Evan was right. He'd suggested leaving Rhys behind, not to gain the upper hand but to save her heart. There was no way she'd put him in harm's way, no way that he'd survive, and if he didn't, then she never would.

"Rhys." She leaned up on her elbow to look into his eyes. "You can't go tomorrow."

"Well then, you have a problem

because you aren't going without me."

"I won't be able to focus if I'm worried about you." She rested in the crook of his arm. "We're dealing with someone that could use mind control on you." She looked up at him. "What if he tells you to kill me? You'd never be able to live with yourself. I won't do that to you."

Rhys slid out of the bed and pulled on his jeans before sitting on the edge of the bed. "Elizabeth, don't do this." He turned and rested his hand on her stomach. "Don't push me away. We're so close to having the life we want. Please, baby."

Elizabeth sat up, letting the covers fall to her waist. She covered his hand. "This is bigger than us, Rhys. All those abducted women need me; they need what the others and I can do in order to save them."

Rhys stood and turned toward her. "Fuck, Elizabeth. I won't stay behind, not if you're in danger. Don't ask me to."

Elizabeth pressed her lips together. She could see the determination in Rhys' eyes. He wasn't going to stay behind. She knew it like she knew herself. No words were going to convince him, no words he wanted to hear.

She swallowed around the lump in her throat as she rose from the bed. "You once told me you'd do anything to make me happy."

She paused, her heart cracking in a million pieces at what she was about to say.

"Lizzie, don't," he growled, knowing what was coming next.

"You have to let me go." She bit the inside of her mouth to stifle any tears. "I'll never be the mate you need or deserve. Never be able to give you a family or be the wife you want. This life isn't for you, but it is for me. I have to do this. I have to be here, you"—she shook her head—"don't."

Her cell phone rang, breaking the silence. She answered it, confused to see Evan's number. "Hanson."

"Meet me in the training room and leave the bear."

She turned her back to Rhys. "Why?"

"Just do it."

"Fine," she answered, turning toward Rhys while she pulled up her jeans and zipped them, "I have to go meet Evan in the training room." She tugged on an oversized shirt. "When I get back, we're finishing the conversation."

"Yeah...we are." He answered as if whatever he might say would change her mind.

She slipped into her boots and shoved a gun in the back of her jeans. Rhys was leaning against the wall, watching her get ready, his arms crossed over his chest, a scowl of disapproval on his face. He reached for her as she opened the door. "There's nothing you can say to me that will make me change my mind. If you're doing this, then I am, too."

Elizabeth walked out, letting the door close behind her. She had to find a way for him to understand. If he got hurt or worse, it would destroy her. Up until now, she'd never had anyone to worry about. Having a mate, even if she couldn't claim him, was going to kill her. She'd always be worried. No, it was better to break things off. He'd stay safe. Even if she'd never be the same, never love another, he'd be safe.

She opened the door to the training room to find Evan standing shirtless in the middle of the floor. Sweat beaded his chest, and his hair was damp and mussed.

"What?" she asked.

"You're making it difficult for me to train."

Her brows dipped. "What the hell are you talking about?"

He pointed to his temple. "I can hear you. I know what's going on, what you're thinking. You're being kind of loud about it, so what's it going to take to get you to go to sleep?"

"Asshole," she grumbled and turned to leave.

He was standing in front of her before she took her first step, he moved with his crazy speed blocking her from leaving. He stepped closer, and she stepped back. They continued the song and dance until he had her in the middle of the room.

"What are you doing?"

Don't hate me for this, he said in her mind as he lifted her arms and wrapped them around his neck. He pulled her against his chest and laid a kiss on her that, had it been Rhys, would have melted her panties. He kissed her like a man starved. The kiss lacked spark and desire, confirming what she already knew. He wasn't her mate.

If you don't stop, I'll kill you, she demanded through their minds, trying to untangle her arms and break the connection.

I'm protecting you and yours in the only way I know how. It's the only way to keep him safe, Evan answered back, breaking the kiss.

Her chest heaved while trying to catch her breath. He turned to look at the door, and she followed his gaze. Rhys was standing in the doorway. His eyes shifted to that of his bear, his shift barely being held in check.

"Is this why you want me to leave? Because you want to be with him?" he asked.

Elizabeth pressed her lips together and swallowed around the lump in her throat.

If she opened her mouth, she'd beg him to stay, and she couldn't, not if it meant losing him in a battle he was ill-equipped to fight. No, she wouldn't speak.

"Answer me, damn it," he growled.

"Rhys, she and I have history and a connection. I tried to explain that to both of you from the very beginning. She just fought the attraction."

He looked at her with hurt and anger in his eyes. A tear slipped free and left a wet path down her cheek. She balled her fist to stop herself from reaching for him, from going to him.

It has to be this way, Lizzie. Stay strong.

"Is it true, Lizzie?"

Kiss me.

No, damn it. I'm already hurting him.

If you don't tell him, he's going to get hurt, Elizabeth. Deal with this now. Give him a reason to walk away.

"I can't deny it." She glanced at Evan. "We do have a connection. We always will," she said, choosing her words wisely. She wouldn't lie to him. Ever.

Rhys gave a slow nod and stepped into Evan's face. He cocked back his fist and swung, hitting him square in the jaw. The power of the punch sent Evan off his feet and to the floor.

Son of a bitch.

Elizabeth dropped to her knees and

cupped Evan's face.

I'm so sorry.

She glanced over her shoulder to find the room empty and Rhys gone.

Elizabeth tried to stand, but Evan grabbed her hand, keeping her from chasing Rhys. "If you go to him, he'll want to fight."

"His safety for a broken heart? Are those my only options?"

"Twenty-four hours, and we'll figure out the rest." Evan rose to his feet and held out a hand to her. "I've got your back. I always have and always will, even where your bear is concerned."

Elizabeth swiped the tears from her eyes and took his outstretched hand. "This sucks."

Evan pulled her up and tossed his arm around her shoulders.

"He's going to leave."

"And you know where to find him when it's over. If you still decide you'd rather have him than me." Evan bumped her shoulder and grabbed two swords from the wall, tossing her one. "Spar? You need to work off your anger?"

She failed miserably at an attempted smile. "I'm going to kick your ass. I owe you for that damn kiss."

"Bring it on, Abigail," Evan teased as he lifted his sword.

Chapter 18

Elizabeth shoved a gun into the waistband of her jeans and used a special belt to hold the paralyzing darts and the royal daggers her father had given her. Emeralds lay embedded in the handles of the deadly weapons. She still wasn't okay with the man and what he'd done, but she didn't have time to dwell on her jacked-up family dynamics. Finding the women took precedence over the anger she harbored.

Evan, Striker, and two of the other Protectors, Kane and Jager, were going with her. They had four more operatives at the lab ready and waiting to join the fight with another team set up at an extraction point. She'd seen their pictures and knew who not to kill. The only people who were walking away were the innocents and her team.

"You look like you lost your puppy," Striker teased, gazing at her through the rearview mirror.

More like her bear. "I'm fine." She turned her gaze back toward the window, watching as the moon rose in the night sky.

She heard Evan in her mind. *Get out of your head. You need to focus.*

Bite me, she answered back. There was no coming back from what she'd deliberately done to Rhys. He'd never forgive her, never trust her again. How was she supposed to fight with that weight on her shoulders?

The SUV pulled off on the side of the road, and they all unloaded, grabbing knives, guns, and their weapons of choice. Hers were her gun, paralyzing darts, and the daggers. Not because her father had given them to her but because they were small and effective.

"We all know the plan. Lizzie, you'll focus on getting the girls and getting them out. We'll handle the rest," Evan announced, his gaze landing on her.

"Get in, get the girls, and get out. I know," she called over her shoulder and started in a jog toward the tree line, not waiting for the others to follow. She sniffed the air. The scent of pine tingled her nose, making it twitch. She dug her boots into the mud, making a path through the trees toward where the satellite images the senator had provided indicated the building sat.

She slowed as she approached the end of the clearing, Evan by her side and the others spread farther out.

The mic in her ear crackled to life with Striker's gravelly voice. "Hold your position. Wait for the signal."

She crouched down in anticipation. Her animals growled loudly in her head, pacing below the surface of her skin. Her gaze was glued to the power box on the side of the building. Two seconds later, the bullet hit. Red sparks flew from the metal, throwing the building into complete darkness. The darkness wasn't an issue for her or the boys and probably not half the shifters in the building, but it knocked out the security, unlocking the doors on their side of the building.

Evan grabbed her arm and used hand signals toward the door. Seconds later, it opened, and a man stepped out, waving them in. She recognized him as one of the inside Protectors that was there to help. Evan stepped into the building first. Her gaze turned a red tint thanks to whichever animal could help her best. She pulled the gun from her waistband, holding it pointed toward the ground as they hurried down the hall, taking several different twists and turns. She'd be lost if the inside agents hadn't provided the layout. She might still get lost trying to get out.

They both slowed, pressing their backs against the wall, moving effectively and efficiently toward their goal, only stopping to peer around the last corner where the hall opened up to where the holding cells were situated. He held up three fingers, and she sniffed the air. *Two wolves and a cat,* she said in her mind.

He nodded and drew his sword. She shook her head, pulling three of the tranquilizers from her belt.

They won't even see me coming, she said.

Gunshots sounded from the opposite direction while screams echoed down the hall.

"Shit, they tripled security. We're hit, and the bastards have us cornered. They're firing tranqs," Striker growled into their ears.

Ambush? she asked.

Evan hesitated, his gaze going back down the hall as he said, *Go help them. I've got this. We'll rendezvous at the SUV.*

He hesitated, but she didn't. She gave him a shove toward the corridor, saying, *In and out, go help the others and pave me a path to the exit.*

He nodded and started jogging down the hallway, leaving the three weres for her to deal with.

I'm not human she reminded herself and tightened the grip on her darts. She peered around the corner and came face to face with a slobbering wolf, baring his pointy yellow teeth. A growl rumbled from deep in his chest. He crouched, and his muscular legs bunched seconds before he jumped on her, knocking her off her feet. She scrambled, using her dragon strength to hold his snout closed as she reached for the nearest dart she'd dropped with his impact and shoved it into the side of his neck. "Sweet dreams."

Seconds later, his large heavy body collapsed on her, and she shoved him to the side while searching the floor for the rest of the darts she'd been holding.

The other two guards were still in human form as they ran around the corner. They stopped and eyed the dog on the ground, giving her time to pull the daggers from behind her back. She didn't wait for them to attack. She used her vampire speed and ran between them, holding each blade at throat level.

She spun as she passed, preparing her stance for another attack. Their bodies fell, blood spurting from their throats.

She pressed the button on her ear com

as she turned. "I'm in."

The room was built like the one holding the cells at her precinct. Ten cells lined both walls with thick metal bars made from silver. Only two were empty, with the doors standing open. She didn't have to guess the human women from the shifters. The humans had tears in their eyes and were clutching the bars. The shifters looked ready to fight.

"Who had the key?" she asked the nearest shifter.

"The wolf," she answered.

Elizabeth glanced over her shoulder back into the hallway, where she should have seen the legs of the wolf she'd jabbed with the dart. He was nowhere to be seen.

"Looks like we're doing this the hard way. Can you shift?"

She shook her head. "No, they pumped us full of some type of sleeping sedative that targets only our animals."

Elizabeth shoved the daggers back into their sheaths and used the strength of her dragon and her immortal speed, yanking the doors off the hinges and throwing them toward the two empty cells. "I'll lead," she hollered over her shoulder as she yanked the last door off.

The missing women were among them.

The last woman was crouched in the corner. Her dirty brunette hair hung in her face.

"Leave her. She'll just slow us down," the woman from the first cell yelled.

"We're all leaving this hellhole," Elizabeth answered. She stepped into the cell and lifted the woman off the ground.

She brushed the hair out of the woman's face and paused. The woman's violet eyes stared back at her, but she still didn't say a word.

Elizabeth guided the woman by her arm leading her to the others. She met the woman's gaze. "You need to keep up." She pushed her will toward the other woman, just to find herself hitting a brick wall.

Elizabeth glanced at one of the other shifters. "Help her."

She left her, moving to the front of the pack. "Stay close, and stay low." She pulled out her gun, holding it in a tight grip in front of her. She moved swiftly down the halls, backtracking toward the exit. She paused at each hallway, taking out a few of the shifters, charging them before ushering the girls past. By the time she got to the end of the hall, her clip was empty, and smoke was filling the halls. She pushed through the door and ran out, the women hot on her heels. They made the tree line, and about half a mile to the extraction point, she yelled to the group. "Head 100 yards north."

"Wait. What about you?" the woman with the violet eyes asked, trying to urge her to continue with them.

"I've got to help the others. Head to the extraction point."

Shots rang out in the night air behind her, coming from the warehouse. "Run, and don't stop."

Elizabeth shoved the gun into her jeans with no bullets left in the chamber. She pulled the daggers off her back and headed back toward the others. She wouldn't leave the others behind if there was a remote chance they needed her help. Ten yards to the clearing, she skidded to a stop. The barrel of a gun pointed at her chest.

"I knew you were going to be a problem," Jennifer Smith sneered. "I told Patrick we hadn't seen the last of you."

"Jennifer?" Elizabeth tightened her hold on the only weapons she had left. The scent of bear made her heart hammer in her chest. The unmistakable smell of Rhys drifted to her nose on the wind. She needed answers before she killed this bitch. Needed to know if there were more labs, more people she would kill. "Why are you doing this?"

"To rid the world of your kind," she smiled. "That's right. My husband told me what you are." She paced to get a better angle. "The General hates shifters as much as I do."

"You're the one behind all of this?"

Elizabeth asked, narrowing her eyes. "No...you aren't, are you? You're not smart enough for this."

"Smart enough to see you coming a mile away. It's a shame I can't kill your animals before watching you die." Jennifer narrowed her eyes and lifted the gun, ready to pull the trigger.

Rhys sprinted from behind a tree, covering Elizabeth's body and blocking her from the weapon as Jennifer pulled the trigger. He grimaced as he held on to her with one hand, using the other to cover the blood pooling out onto his shirt.

"She's using silver bullets." He grimaced. His words were whispered. "I love you."

"No...." the woman screamed. "That was meant for her."

Elizabeth didn't wait another second. She used her strength to propel the dagger, slicing it through the air, and the silver landed directly in the woman's chest. The gun fell from her hand, and Jennifer gripped the handle as if to pull the dagger free.

"Not this time." Elizabeth threw the other dagger, embedding the blade into the woman's brain. Her body dropped to the ground.

"Rhys." Elizabeth eased him over. His eyes were closed, and his head lolled to the side. She felt for a pulse. It was faint beneath her fingertips.

Evan, she screamed in her head. *He's dying.*

Seconds passed that seemed like minutes. She'd shoved up her sleeve, ready to open her vein and have him feed from her as a last resort, when Evan appeared by her side, moving her out of the way to get a better look.

"No, you'll kill him. He's not immortal."

"The bullet was silver. He's dying," she breathed out with tears streaking down her face. She watched in horror as Evan ripped Rhys' shirt open.

"Good thing we're immune." He glanced up at her. "I have to change him. He'll be just like us. Well, just like me."

She nodded. "Save him."

Evan gave her the royal nod before using his teeth to slice open his wrist. He held it to Rhys' mouth. She heard Evan order Rhys to drink. Evan's face became paler as Rhys took more enzymes from his blood. He didn't have enough.

Elizabeth shoved up her sleeve and held her own wrist to Evan's mouth.

He turned his face.

"If you don't save him, we'll both die." She held his gaze. "I won't live without him, and you're tied to me." She shoved her wrist to his mouth.

His teeth clamped down on her inner arm, and she dropped to her knees and lifted her head to the stars in the night sky. She felt her life force draining. Her eyes slid closed. Her body was heavy as the darkness sucked her into a black void.

Chapter 19

Elizabeth sat up with a start, letting out a quick breath as she remembered the vision of Rhys lying near death on the forest floor.

"It's okay," Evan said, calming her and easing her back down onto the bed. "You're safe."

She gazed around the unfamiliar room. "Where am I?"

"The infirmary." Evan eased down on her bed.

"Where's Rhys?"

Evan shifted his gaze to the bed on the other side of her, and she turned. Rhys had IVs sticking in his arm, attached to hanging bags of red liquid. The same stuff she'd drunk the last time she'd lost too many enzymes. Monitors displayed his vitals.

"Why isn't he awake?" she asked, trying to sit up again, only to be stopped by Evan, who pressed a lever on the bed, raising the head portion so she could see.

"The transformation takes time, Lizzie." Evan's voice was quiet.

She turned back to Evan. "What happened? Did everyone make it out?"

Her heart clenched, and she swallowed around her sore throat.

Sensing her pain, Evan handed her a glass of the red liquid. "We salvaged what we could from the warehouse in an attempt to find Raw, and the women are safe." He pressed his lips together.

"What about the woman with the violet eyes? Have you figured out who she is? I tried to push my will on her to keep up, and she blocked me."

His brows dipped. "She doesn't remember who she is or even how she ended up at the compound."

Evan's gaze softened as he pushed the hair behind her ear. "You saved him." He ran his hand over the pink mark on her arm where Evan had bitten her.

"He saved me first," she said, glancing over to her mate. Hell, would he even want her when he realized what they'd done? Did he even want to be immortal? "Let's just hope he wanted this."

Evan cupped her face, turning her to

look at him. "He's a lucky man."

"You're going to be a dead one if you don't remove your hand," Rhys growled from his bed and grabbed his throat.

Lizzie slid her legs over the side of the bed and stood, pulling her hanging bag with her. She took the crimson drink and lifted it to his mouth as she held his head. "This makes the pain go away."

He drank until the cup was empty.

Elizabeth glanced over her shoulder to find Evan had left and they were alone in the room.

"Don't hate me," she whispered and cupped his cheek. "I wanted to keep you safe."

"I could never hate my mate. I figured out what you'd done five minutes after I left, but those assholes wouldn't let me back in." He pushed himself to sit up before pulling her into his lap. "I love you. I'll always love you."

A tear slipped from her eye. "I love you, too."

He crashed his lips to hers in an immortal force he'd yet to control. His passionate kiss was different now, more intense since he'd been turned. His lips on her mouth set off fireworks in her core. Everything was magnified tenfold. The kiss, the feel, the emotions coursing through her body hit with the force of a tidal wave, ready to pull them back out to sea from the safety of the shore.

She broke the kiss.

His lust-filled eyes stared back at her, his gaze intent. "I could get used to that."

She smiled. "Not until we're both well."

"And preferably when you have a room with a door and walls," her father announced, walking into the room. "Glad you're safe." He glanced at Elizabeth before stopping at the end of the bed.

"Rhys." Her father gave a royal nod to her mate. "You saved my Ab— Elizabeth, and for that, I give you my blessing."

Elizabeth tilted her head, unsure what the hell the old man was talking about. "Blessing for what?"

He glanced up from their joined hands to Elizabeth. His face softened. "Now that he's immortal, you can complete the mating bond without killing him."

"Hate to break it to you, old man, but I don't need your blessing. I've gone my whole life without it, and I'll live the rest of my life the same way."

"Lizzie, give him a chance," Rhys said softly. "He's the reason you were born. He's the reason I found you, and he's the reason that we can finally be together."

Her heart skipped a beat, and her belly fluttered as she squeezed Rhys' hand, but she still couldn't let go of the anger toward her father, not without him feeling the same pain.

"Rhys, I know you think I need him, but I don't. I only need you. I"—she swallowed around the lump in her throat—"can't forgive him."

"Baby, I know this is hard, but in the end, you'll thank me." He glanced up at the king. "Hurt her again, and I'll kill you myself."

"How dare you." The king bristled.

"With all due respect, sir, you did this to yourself. If this is the best she can do, you have to accept that. A wise friend once told me that, with your daughter, trust had to be earned. If you want a relationship with her, then I suggest you start trying, because crown or not, I won't let you hurt her again. I may not be related by blood, but I *am* her family, and I will protect her, even if that means protecting her from you."

Seconds that seemed like minutes ticked by before her father spoke again. His voice softened. "Glad to hear you say that." He paused. "Because when you complete the bond, you'll be her protector. Evan will have fulfilled his duties, and the connection between Evan and Elizabeth will be severed."

"What?" Lizzie asked, unsure she'd heard him correctly. "I thought there was no way to break the tie. He would have told me."

Her father pressed his lips together.

"Of course he didn't tell you. He knew you would never be able to complete the mating bond with Rhys or anyone else. He'd never leave you alone and unprotected. Ever."

Her heart fell into her stomach, and she looked down at her hands. He was always supposed to be in her life. In the short time, she'd known him, he had been the only one besides Rhys who attempted to understand. What was life going to be like without Evan in it? She'd come to care for him, maybe not as a mate, but as a friend. Would he even consider her a friend if it weren't mandated? She could hear her father's heavy step as he left without another word, letting her ponder what would be.

Rhys used the crook of his finger to lift her gaze. "Lizzie. I'm sorry, baby. I know you care about him."

She swallowed, and a tear slid down her cheek.

"I'm thankful he's been there for you." He brushed his lips across hers in a heartfelt kiss, making her close her eyes. Another tear slipped free.

"I need to talk to him." She opened her eyes. "Either way, he'll be crushed or elated. Whatever his reaction, it's going to hurt me."

No need to tell me. You already did, Evan said into her mind. *I'm due for a vacation. Lizzie, it's better this way. You love him, and he'll make you happy.*

Evan...

I just need some time. Goodbye, Lizzie.

Don't go, she pleaded. *Let me help you.*

****

Evan didn't answer back. No matter how many times she called for him in her head, the answer was always the same. He was silent.

Elizabeth took one last look in the bathroom mirror and gave herself a sad smile. Butterflies flitted in her belly at the thought of completing the bond with Rhys. He made her happy, yet she knew the minute she bit him her connection with Evan would be forever gone. One more try. One more final goodbye. She had to try.

This is your last chance, you stubborn ass. I won't hear you again. I love Rhys with every fiber of my being, Evan, and I can't change that, but you and I....it wasn't supposed to end this way. I miss your friendship. I miss you.

Silence greeted her as she gripped the sink tighter and lowered her head. Her shoulders deflated while waiting and hoping that he'd reply.

Go bite your mate already and get out of my head, Abigail.

Her eyes popped open, and a small

smile tilted on her lips at him calling her the name meant to aggravate her.

Asshole.

Takes one to know one, princess.

Elizabeth rested her hand on the knob, knowing that this was the last intimate conversation she'd ever have with the man who was tied to her soul.

Quit stalling, he teased. *I'm ready for the silence.*

She grinned and turned the knob.

One more thing, Lizzie. There was a pause. *We'll always be connected even if I'm no longer your protector and can't hear your thoughts. I think everyone is forgetting that I turned you into an immortal. We'll always have that bond. I'll always have your back, no matter what, princess. You can count on it. Now go be happy. You damn well deserve it.*

You do, too. I hope you find love and peace, Evan. Wherever that may be.

I'll be seeing you, Queenie.

Elizabeth chuckled. *Asshole.*

Always.

Elizabeth pulled the door open to find Rhys lying on the bed. Worry clouded his gaze. "Did he answer this time?"

She smiled and nodded.

"About damn time. I thought I was going to have to hunt him down and kick his ass." He smiled up at her and held out his hand. Her life would never be the same after tonight.

She crawled up onto the bed and into his arms. Rhys leaned over her and pressed a tender kiss to her lips. "This isn't the end, baby. It's just the beginning."

"I love you," she whispered against his lips. "I'll love you forever."

Rhys cupped her cheek with his warm palm. "I was born to love you, Elizabeth. You're my family, and bite or not, that will never change." He held her gaze. "I'll still protect and love you, always, even without the bond."

Rhys' eyes gleamed with love. He meant every word. She knew it like she knew how to breathe. This man was her world and would always be. No matter what obstacles life threw her way, there was no one else she wanted by her side. Her man, her mate.

"I'm yours, only yours," she whispered and watched as his bear's eyes flashed back.

"As I'm yours, my mate," he answered before crushing his lips to hers..

Text KATE to 313131 and get a text message on release dates!

Sign up for her newsletters at
www.kateallenton.com

Other Books by Kate Allenton

Suggested Reading Order

BENNETT SISTERS BOX SET (Books 1-4 in one bundle, 1218 pages)

INTUITION (Book 1)

TOUCH OF FATE (Book 2)

MIND PLAY (Book 3)

THE RECKONING (Book 4)

REDEMPTION (Book 5)

CHANCE ENCOUNTERS (Book 6)

DESTINED HEARTS (Book 7)

PHANTOM PROTECTORS BOX SET (Books 1-4 in one bundle, 964 pages)

RECKLESS ABANDON (Book 1)

BETRAYAL (Book 2)

UNTAMED (Book 3)

GUIDED LOYALTY (Book 4)

CARRINGTON-HILL INVESTIGATIONS

DECEPTION (Book 1)

DEADLY DESIRE (Book 2)

SHIFTER PARADISE BOX SET

NOT MY SHIFTER/ SINFULLY CURSED

SOPHIE MASTERSON SERIES/ DIXON SECURITY

LIFTING THE VEIL (Book 1)

BEYOND THE VEIL (Book 2)

VEILED INTENTIONS (Book 3)

VEILED THREATS (Book 4)

THE LOVE FAMILY SERIES

SKYLAR (BOOK1)

DECLAN (BOOK 2)

FLYNN (BOOK 3)

REED (BOOK 4)

LANDON (BOOK 5)

ALEXIS (BOOK 6)

GABE (BOOK 7)

JACKSON (BOOK 8)

LINKED INC.

DEADLY INTENT (BOOK 1)

PSYCHIC LINK (BOOK 2)

PSYCHIC CHARM (BOOK 3)

PSYCHIC GAMES (BOOK 4)

DEADLY DREAMS (BOOK 5)

Stand Alone Books

HELL BOUND

KARMA

MYSTIC TIDES BOX SET

MYSTIC LUCK BOX SET

About the Author

Kate has lived in Florida for most of her entire life. She enjoys a quiet life with her husband, Michael and two kids.

Kate has pulled all-nighters finishing her favorite books and also writing them. She says she'll sleep when she's dead or when her muse stops singing off key.

She loves creating worlds full of suspense, secrets, hunky men, kick ass heroines, steamy sex and oh yeah the love of a lifetime. Not to mention an occasional ghost and other supernatural talents thrown into the mix.

She loves to hear from her readers by email at KateAllenton@hotmail.com, on Twitter@KateAllenton, and on Facebook at facebook.com/kateallenton.1

Visit her website at www.kateallenton.com

Visit Coastal Escape Publishing's website at www.coastalescapepublishing.com